Harbor Excursions

RITA SLANINA

Thank you! Thousand Oaks Library

Acknowledgements

Thank you to all my family and friends that supported me throughout the duration of this book. This is just the beginning. Thank you to my editor for fixing me. A special thank you to the guy who helped take our author photo. My son, I love you so much. And huge gratitude to the other guy who let us use that backdrop for said photo. You have my heart and you always know how to make me laugh.

CONTENTS

1

Chapter One

The hotel called was bustling. Phones ringing. Guests moving in and around through the halls. The main floor bar was full of patrons, enjoying laughs. The city of San Diego had a constant buzz of engaging people, rustling, and on the go. Vacation resorts, news media inviting those not residing here enticing them to visit this beautiful city. At the entrance floor of the hotel, there were bellhops ready to move guests' luggage to the rooms, registration attendants in a fuss to accommodate each guest quickly in a friendly manner. When Johannes stepped into the crowded elevator his mind was sharp, in focus.

He had a late night business meeting and he needed to set some colleagues straight. They were messing with a delicate account, and he didn't want to lose it. This would be his biggest account yet, and would bring him worldwide exposure in the television media. This was the kind of account he was working so diligently hard for all his life. He wasn't going to let others stand in the way of this one. He rode the elevator to the top floor, appropriately called The Top of the Hyatt where the nightlife could find drinks and atmosphere at their fingertips. He entered the bar area, where his associates flagged him to their table. As he strode over to the table, Out of the corner of his eye, he noticed a gorgeous woman at the bar, he kept on towards his table, and attempted to remain focused on the business matter at hand.

Johannes Oxenburg was tall, dark, and handsome. He had broad shoulders, and a statuesque look to his face. His cheekbones were chiseled, and his eyes demanding yet charming. His smile was devilish, but perfect. His dark loose hair softened him a bit, while his physique carried him lean and muscular. He came from a well to-do English family. He sipped tea at high noon, always dressed appropriately and never failed to properly greet everyone he met. He was from the wealthy parts of Great Britain. He was bred to be distinguished, and always to be lavish. He had moved to San Diego as an adult to busy himself with business affairs to great success. He loved San Diego, with its beautiful nighttime skyline and busy city streets. He often rode the trolley to read his paper, and visit the beach side restaurants for his breakfasts. While all his current events in business were on the up and up, and couldn't help but sense he now wanted more. Running his investment firm, keeping a tight ship with everyone around him was exciting, and he always yearned for more of that; however, he was getting to the point in his life where he wanted more. He wasn't thinking about having a family, he was far too self-centered for that. When he saw this beautiful woman sitting alone at the Top of the Hyatt lounge, he couldn't help but wonder how someone so beautiful, so magnificent could be left to her lonesome. An evening business meeting? A date with some bloke who obviously didn't deserve her company. She was beautiful. Long, wavy, auburn hair, a perfect athletic shape. She was wearing these beautifully detailed shoes which are telltale to him of a woman who knows what she likes, wants, and probably usually gets. From quick glances her nails he could barely see but noticed were manicured to perfection.

"Johannes," one of his guests announced. "Johannes! Are you with us here? " Here for a late meeting himself, he was brought back from his rampant thoughts of that stunning vision abruptly.

"Ah, yes, I believe that if we plan our attack to seal the deal with Mr. Lockon, we must prove intense gander and splendid efforts," Johannes responded to his colleagues in hopes that he was, at least, half aware of what the current topic of conversation was momentarily.

"I was asking you what we were planning for the annual gathering for all the members of the firm, Johannes" His business acquaintance, and longtime friend Gary sternly stated. After a short pause, he leaned closer and whispered, "you know...I respect you Johannes. As a business man, and as a longtime friend. But, lately you've been distracted. Are you in need of a friend's ear? I'm always here for you."

Johannes cut in, "Gary, I'm fine. Now isn't the time to discuss such matters. Now I haven't given the annual gathering much thought, but come up with something and run it by me next week. It's closing in on us, and I want the firm to walk away from it so ecstatic about their working environment that it will catch wind across shorelines. Something that will bring businessmen at the top of their game to our company."

"Very well then. And, the Lockon account, what's the deadline on that?"

"Get some brainstorming done this week, and let's meet Friday morning bright and early to go over what you got, and then I want a formal presentation ready by Monday , eight a.m. sharp."   "Alright. I have a meeting with his assistant Gayle Lockharte. I hear she's quite a looker," Gary said with bright interested eyes.

"Settle down there cowboy. She's quite a vulture if you don't watch yourself. I suggest you keep your eyes on the prize. And by that I don't mean on her, I mean the account. Are we understood?" Johannes had a brief run-in with Gayle Lockharte years ago while she was dating an old colleague. His first impression of her was just not a positive one. He always felt she was the type of person to dig for gold. And, if a man wasn't loaded with it, she would get out quick and leave nothing but a dust cloud in her tracks.

The men nodded in subtle amusement and all rose out of their chairs to leave. Shook hands and bade farewell. Meanwhile, in Johannes wiry mind, he was acutely focused on the woman at the bar. Was she still seated there? Had she gone? If so, in which direction? As soon as he found the last sight of his colleagues turn the corner, he whipped his head around in her direction at the bar. With a sigh of nervous relief, he saw her, still there. Still waiting on someone? He had hoped not. Johannes took a deep breath and started heading towards the bar. As he sat next to her, he flagged the bartender to order himself a drink. Not because he was thirsty, but because he didn't want to look too eager to talk to her, and probably calm his nerves a little bit. Out of the corner of his eye, he could see her take a swift glance in his direction, and without purpose he attempted to smile and make eye contact. To no avail. Her head turned away so quickly, he had to question whether she even looked at him, or if he had imagined it. As the thoughts raced through his mind, the bartender had brought his drink. A vodka tonic. He needed to relax. He took a drink, then set down the glass gently. Closed his eyes as he drew in another deep breath, and exhaled.

"Rough day?" The woman asked. Surprised, and elated that she spoke to him, Johannes sort of stood there in a lost state of sorts. The woman, unsure of what possible boundary she may have crossed, quickly readdressed him, "I'm sorry, I didn't realize you may have wanted to be alone, excuse me." She started to get down off her chair, and Johannes reached for her arm.

"No-I mean, I'm sorry for my rudeness, and no, I do not want to be alone. Oh, that didn't come out right either." Johannes responded with embarrassment. He realized he was talking too fast, and too much. His thoughts were moving along ten times faster than his mouth, and he stopped short. And with a chuckle he said, "I'm Johannes Oxenburg. I usually don't fumble so profusely. And you are?" She gave a smirk, and sat back down. "It's alright. I'm Miranda. Miranda Setes. I come here on occasion to let off a little steam, give myself a break from the 'norm' I guess you can say"

He couldn't help but feel compelled to just wrap her up in his arms and whisk her away to the top suite of the luxurious hotel. Taste her, titillate her. How could he feel this way? He only saw her from across the room. He's a serious, and practical man. Not caught up in love at first site fairy tales, and imagined goddesses. What is this feeling coming over him? And while he did not know, nor understand it, he didn't care. He wanted to have her, to make her his. Her beautiful face, her mysterious eyes, and while he hadn't made it obvious, he sure did see her perfect body silhouetted atop the chair. Catching himself droning on and on, he quickly started in, " I own an investment firm here in the city. I don't find it easy to catch time for myself to blow off any steam. I have very demanding clients. Or rather, I'm just a very pricey decision maker/babysitter for grown men! So, what about yourself? "

She gave a wry smile, and she felt compelled to sort of fib her way through this one. She didn't believe her husband would know this man, but nonetheless, she opted to keep such facts hidden momentarily. Since he himself was, at least in the business of investing. She could only assume a probability that her own husband may have inquired about his services, or at some point may. The thought of just keeping her marriage a secret for the time being might be in the best interest for the both of them. "Oh, I don't do much really. I am involved in the community. I started a charitable organization that benefits young orphaned children called Kid Dreams. I enjoy giving back, and that takes a lot of my time. Well, enough about me, how does your wife handle your long hours?" She proposed the question in hopes of getting a response from him. He didn't seem to be married, he isn't wearing a wedding band, and earlier when he was noticing her from across the room, she noticed him gazing longer than someone just observing his surroundings. She sensed an interest from him, and she was definitely interested in him. "Oh, " he said with a chuckle, " I'm not married. Oh no. I haven't had the time for it in my life, and frankly you women can tend to complicate matters..."

"Is that right?" She said with a disapproving, yet jovial eye, "Are we a bit jaded?" "Think about it, when you want to leave your home for an evening out, can you just go without your significant other giving you the where are you going, what are you doing, when you coming home bit? Please, I need my sanity," he said with humorous conviction. "I suppose your right, although what about those moments of silence, while your basking in your solitude? Wouldn't be nice to have someone there for you no matter what, read the paper next to you, snuggle when it's chilly? I'm convinced you believe you have been castrated, and aren't planning an endeavor of sorts anytime soon"

"Well, slow down now, I didn't say all that. I was just merely pointing out the nuisances of a relationship that can drive you to the slow death of your sanity. I'm kidding. I would like to find her one day, but it all comes down to timing, and meeting the right one." Clamoring to make him a bit uneasy, she asked, "Do you think we ever meet the right one? I mean, it all seems a bit fantasy."

"You don't believe in meeting the right one?" "Well, I don't know. Have you ever been in a relationship and after a time it has gone dry, and dull?" "Sure, we all have at some-" "Well, I guess that is what affected my belief , or rather disbelief in meeting 'the one.'" Miranda said sternly. She couldn't help but wonder on about such a topic of conversation. She's known this man one minute, and we're already talking about meeting the one? Maybe she's said too much. Maybe she's rambled on, or scared him off rather. She believed in what she was saying. Didn't she? Certainly he can't be the one, she's married to 'the one.' Oh, but his luscious lips that words escape in such a sexy British accent.. Startled away from her thoughts, she heard him say something. "I'm sorry, what?" "Let's change the topic. Why are you sitting here all alone? Are you waiting for someone?"

"Oh no. I come here on occasion to release my thoughts. To sort of relax my anxieties." "Want to talk about any of those thoughts and anxieties? I'm all ears, should you need a pair," he said with slight jest. "I was here for a business meeting with my colleagues. Had to boss some people around." They both laughed at his joke. "So, how long have you been in the states?" Miranda asked. "Oh," he chuckled, "Quite a while now. Too long to count really." Miranda picked up her glass, still almost full with her dirty martini. Johannes watched as she delicately sipped from the cloudy glass. Her lips pursed, her fingers so gently wrapping the stem of the glass. Her other hand softly pinching the olive skewer, keeping it from sliding into her delicate face. Taking in every moment, he found himself breathing slightly heavily. As she placed her martini back to the counter, he put his hand on her forearm. And before he could stop himself from probably messing this up, he found himself saying, "Could we--I mean," slowing his pace, "would you let me see you again sometime?"

"Well, my new, dear friend, if we should run into each other again, so be it." With that she gave a wry smile, grabbed her purse and got up to leave. "I will be here again soon." He wasn't sure what the heck she meant by that, but apparently this woman was going to be a challenge for him. And boy, did he love a challenge.

2

Chapter Two

Johannes was sitting at his desk in his office unable to concentrate. It had been three weeks since he saw her. Miranda. Her name kept running through his mind to exhaustion. He had gone back to the Top of the Hyatt four different times in an attempt to see her again. How could he let her go without getting her phone number? She had him so caught up in the moment of her timelessness that he wasn't very smooth in actions, nor did he think clearly enough to get the information he so desperately wanted from her. He had to forget her. And in that moment, he definitely tried. Luckily, for sanity's sake, his friend and colleague Gary entered his office. Gary Solden had been friends with Johannes since Johannes moved here from England. Johannes had answered an ad for a room for rent, and they shared that apartment for many years. They hung out together, swapped stories, fought about who should be cleaning up the dishes. Johannes being from his wealthy background was not accustomed to cleaning up after his own messes since he had the help of multiple housekeepers to do that for him back home. Nonetheless, with reluctance, he complied with the common house rules. Gary introduced him to a man named Victor Setes. Mr. Setes then introduced Johannes to the game of investing. When Johannes felt that he was strong enough to compete with the other firms, he then opened his own firm, and became known as the man who makes it happen. People fight for weeks; sometimes, months, just to get an appointment with him. He's at the top of his game and though he never ran into Mr. Setes after his humble beginnings branched into his current position of greatness, he was sure he was fine. That man was very, very wealthy. He hadn't needed to work -ever. Johannes owes a lot to Gary. For being the great friend he was, and still is. If it wasn't for meeting Gary, neither of them would be where they are today.

"So, I met with Ms. Lockharte..." he took deep excited sigh. "Alright Gary. So, what did you come up with for the Lockon account?" "She kept asking me questions about you," as he pulled out a chair and sat down across from Johannes. "Really," taking a disconcerted pause, "were you two talking business or was she fishing for a new husband?" "She used to date Mr. Lockon. Apparently they met a few years back, got to talking, one thing led to another, and she's his number one producing commercial realtor. She also gave me a few historic stories and kept switching back to you."

Aggravated, Johannes snipped, "Gary, the account specifics, please." After a brief pause, he continued, "Wait, what? What foolishness are you getting to already?" "Oh, no. Nothing, nothing at all. I just found it odd that she kept questioning me about you, that's all." "Alright," changing the subject as quickly as he could. The last thing he needed was a woman's interest intruding on a huge account like this one. "So, professionally, what did she present were her -or rather Mr. Lockon's concerns, and issues were? And from that meeting, were you able to get an informal presentation together for me to look over?"

"Yes. Here are the graphs on our projected financial gains, over costs. Here's my proposal, and oh, Gayle wanted me to get this to you, here's her number. She said should you have any questions, feel free to call her directly."

"Why? Did you drool all over her or something?" Johannes said chuckling. " No, that's all she told me to tell you." Sighing to avoid any further irritation brought on by this man today, "Thank you Gary. I'll get these back to you with my revisions by this afternoon." Standing up, Gary moved around to the backside of the chair, pushing it back into its place. "You know, you're not going to see her again." They reached to shake hands to bid farewell. "What?" Startled and confused, his mind raced. "What are you talking about?" He was sure he saw all his business associates leave that night at the Top of the Hyatt.

"That woman you were talking to. After our business meeting earlier a few weeks ago. You were acting a little strange that night, and so after I made sure everyone got to their cars, I went back up to the bar to see if you were alright. When I went back in, I saw you sitting with a woman. You looked like you were nervous as hell, but I figured you were just doing you, so I didn't want to interrupt. I would ask you if you took her home that night, "he said smirking, " but, I already know the answer to that."

"It's not what you think. She-" "That's what I meant by, you're not going to see her again. One night stands. They're like that. Sometimes they work out to something more-"

"It wasn't like that Gary." Feeling his temper flaring by the insinuations protruding from his friend's mouth. Sure, in the past he was definitely the lady's man. A run around town type of guy, but not since the woman he actually fell in love with. No, it was different with her. She was so beautiful and perfect, similar in being to Miranda. "Look Gary, she didn't -I didn't take her home with me. We went our separate ways, and that was that." He failed to mention that he has since returned every night at the same place to hopefully see her again.

"Wait, wait, wait! Are you kidding me? The man who ran with a different woman every other night, is telling me that he *didn't* take this one home?! I'm astonished!"

"Come on, you know I haven't dated since..." he trailed off, and looked back at his desk.

"I know, and it's about time you did, don't you think? Hey, there's Gayle's number, use it. If anything, you get yourself a good time!" He said winking. Johannes nodded his head, and returned to his paperwork on the Lockon account. Maybe he should call Gayle. What are the chances that he would see Miranda again anyhow? If she was interested wouldn't she have given him her number? A date? Something? With all the rumors he's heard about Gayle though, he wasn't so sure he was that interested in her. Something about Gayle did not sit well with him. He knew she got the job by boyfriend, and as far as he could tell she was still blowing him. You don't walk around in designer labels, and $15,000 necklaces if you're not blowing your rich boss. He held her number in his hand, gave it one more thought, then tossed it in his desk drawer. He didn't know whether he was going to use it or not, but he wasn't ready to throw out her number either.

He finished up his revisions on the account, placed it in an envelope, and as he left the office he placed it on Gary's desk. By the way, where was Gary? He remembered telling Gary he'd be dropping off the revision for him to formalize. This account was far too important to have a frivolous attitude. Just then he heard giggling coming from the reception. He headed towards it and saw Gary's arm on the counter, and a glimpse of a woman's frame behind his. "Oh no," he mumbled under his breath. Gayle Lockharte. As quickly as he realized who was standing there, he tried to turn around, and then he was spotted.

"Oh, Johannes! Johannes! There you are. I wanted to reach you before I went away for the weekend," Gayle said excitedly. "Could we step into your office for some privacy?"

Gary gave Johannes a thumbs up from behind Gayle's back, and all Johannes could do was try to escape. "I was actually on my way out, if you need assistance, Gary has the proposal on his desk, in fact, I just dropped it on his desk."

Oh, no, I am actually here on a personal visit," she motioned towards an office, "Shall we?"

"Sure Ms. Lockharte," he guided her to the back into his office. "How did you know what floor I was on?" "Oh, I just asked Mr. Lockon. He knows everything, he's so smart."

Gayle was a beautiful young lady. Too young to be so successful in this market, but nonetheless definitely young. She had long flowing blond hair, and a petite frame. Her business attire was not so business though. Her blouse was a see-thru nude-colored lace material, which showed the shape of her round perky breasts. Slightly large for her frame. Her skirt was a little on the short side exposing her shapely legs, and her high heels were stilettos with a silver metal heel. He watched as she swayed her hips from side to side, walking one foot in front of the other. He could see why Mr. Lockon showed an interest in her. Wondering what on earth she was doing here in his office, and dressed so scantily clad, he just couldn't fathom going out with her. Not that he thought she was out of his league-but rather he was out of hers. But since he's obviously lost his chance with Miranda, maybe he could look at other options. As he shut the door behind them, he turned to her, and asked, "To what do I owe the pleasure Ms. Lockharte."

"Oh, please, Johannes, call me Gayle. There's no need for formalities between us. I stopped by to see if you were available to accompany me this weekend. Mr. Lockon has an estate he's been eyeing for purchase. Since you seem to know him well in business, I thought maybe you'd have some insight on his personal tastes."

"Ms. Lockharte-" "Gayle." She said assertively.

"Gayle, I don't really seem to feel comfortable with that offer. I spoke with Mr. Lockon recently, and he had not mentioned needing my opinion seeming to matter on his own personal purchases. If you have other intentions, I am not interested."

"You're quick. I do have other intentions. But, since I am to be there all weekend, I would much rather have a friend." She moved closer to him, making him a little uneasy. She teased his collar with her perfectly manicured nails. Raising an eyebrow, and giving a come-hither smile, she leaned in a little closer to his face. Mouth to mouth, almost touching, and she whispered, "You know, a little sleepover. Doesn't that sound like fun?" Unsure of what to do, he put his hands to her shoulders, and gently backed away from her. "I don't believe this would be appropriate, besides, if I'm not mistaken, aren't you and Mr. Lockon-"

"Yes, we are." She said as a matter of fact, "But that has nothing to do with us here, now does it?"

Stuck in a state of shock, he could feel a rise out of his pants. All he could do was try to calm himself down, and figure out how to get out of the situation, but before he could think on this a little further, she had leaned in and kissed him firmly on the mouth. She wrapped her leg around his, using her stiletto heel to flirt with his inner calf. He kissed her back, and immediately flung her around, putting her on top the desk. Aggressively their tongues played in each other's mouths, he fingered her hair with his hands, while she started to unbutton his shirt. He took off his blazer and threw it to the floor, and lifted her blouse to expose her big, beautiful breasts. He leaned down to suck on them, and taste the sweet flesh of this beautiful creature. She reached for his pants and undid them. He lifted himself onto her, feeling his manhood pulsate with each thrust. She sank her nails into his back, throwing her head back with satisfaction. With each lustful kiss, he entered her harder, feeling her tightening around his throbbing cock. Together they staked claim on their orgasms -explosive, and breathless.

They each reached for their clothes, and pulled themselves together. Gayle quickly fixed her hair, gave one swipe of lip gloss to her lips, and gave Johannes a quick peck on the cheek. "Nice chat we had, thanks!" And with that, she bounced out the door glancing back at him and added a wink.

*   *   *   *

At his home, sitting in his library amongst the crop of aged books, he took a swig of his drink. He always liked his Jack & Coke, but today he felt drawn to a straight whiskey. He had now a luxurious home on the waterfront. Everything decorated to the tee (hilt). No expense spared. His ideal home had to have oceanic views, and top of the line furnishings. Johannes sure had come a long way from his studio apartment he once shared. And when he could finally afford it, he went all out. Leaning back in his imported Italian leather chair, he propped his feet up on its matching ottoman, thumbing through the pages of his current read.

As he sat intensely laboring over his mind's inability to focus on the words on the pages. Thoughts raced back through the day's earlier events. "How could that woman seduce me? I know myself better than that; Yet, I allowed her to coerce me..." He thought aloud. With a disgruntled sigh, he arose out of his chair, and thwarted toward the telephone. "I will phone her, and explain that it was a huge mistake and that there is no point in continuing this escapade...but, that wouldn't be right, what escapade? One time doesn't make it a 'thing", or make us an item...." Johannes' deliberation continued. Then once again. Aloud, he restated to himself, "It was nothing.

It's over and done. What's happened has happened. Gary will deal with her from here on out, and there will be nothing to worry about." And with that affirmation to himself, he found his contemplation move onto another subject that was troubling him.

3

Chapter Three

At lunch with her childhood friend, Miranda sits with Josie discussing their lives as most women dining together tend to do. As the waiter brings their food, Josie is rambling on about the recent engagement, the gifts he's bought her, and so on. Miranda sits in her thoughts, pondering days gone by when she welcomed the chime of happiness that rings when women become engaged. Her marriage was once so happy. How did I get here? She thought. I've been married to the same man for years now, and as it had gone stale, I took the appropriate measures to spice things up. I took it upon myself to lift his spirits up when the stock market had its huge fall. I put myself to exhaustion in my quest to keep him happy, and lose my own sense of self in the process. She placed her napkin on her lap slowly. What happened to Miranda? What happened to me? A cloudy gaze was across her face as she was deep in contemplation, when she was shook by the eerie sound of Josie's voice.

"Miranda. Miranda. Miranda!" laughing, "Where are you girl? Earth to my little chick-a-dee!"

"Oh, sorry. " Miranda quivered, startled.

"You were doing it again. The 'lost in space' look."

With a short chuckle Miranda replied, "Sorry. I have just been so wrapped up in so many things lately, that I can't keep focused one tiny bit." Hoping that covered up her staged happiness, she lifted her fork and began to work on her entree. "I just love when they put little tangerines and slivered almonds atop of salad. It really gives it a surprising flair."

Staring at her with astonishment, as if she cannot believe that her best friend of twenty-some odd years actually believes she pawned that off on her, Josie sits and stares at Miranda with her jaw open. "You're kidding me right?" A diminutive pause later, "You mean to tell me. That my friend Miranda. After an eon of friendship. Is actually daring to assert herself as the queen of 'fine'? And, affirms unto herself only, that I believe you are fine? Come on, what's really going on? You have been neither here nor there for months on end, and I just can't take it anymore." In an aggravated whisper she continues, "if you don't come clean and tell me what's up, I'm going to...to...eat up all your salad, with all that flair you're trying to convince me of!" Josie stabs at Miranda's salad with angst, and bites down, chewing harshly. Drops the fork to the table, and folds her arms with an heir of "your move sister."

As they both softly boast with glee, Miranda sets her own fork to the table, much more gracefully than Josie just had, and inhales a ready-deserved, deep sigh. "Victor and I have been having problems."

"I knew it!"

"No, not problems, per say, but we are just moving apart. Well, no, not that either. I don't know, that's why I haven't spoken of it." With hesitation, Josie responds boldly, "Not problems. Not moving apart. Not connecting. I don't get it, then what's the problem?" "That's just it, I don't know. He's not acting any differently. Victor has always worked late, so that's nothing new to me. I just honestly cannot put my finger on it. We're moving into our years together where I believe we should be spending it vacationing, or just lounging on a porch somewhere enjoying the peace and quiet."

"Do you think he's having an affair?"

"Oh come on Josie. I won't hear of something so ridiculous. Why is it when people question their relationships, the first thing people have to say is, are they having an affair? Really, Victor and I decided and agreed long ago, that if things became latent between us on his or my side of it we would have the courtesy and respect to let one another know of it, and without disgruntlement would free each other. If it had to come to such a resolution," Miranda said this in such a convincing, dignified manner, that even she had to trace back over her steps and accept how eloquently she delivered that.

"Look Miranda, that may be so, and you may have it all figured out, the both of you; But, honestly, after so many years, sometimes the person you married, ends up being someone else entirely. Someone you don't even know. You can never be too sure, and I know, you are right. I should not presume that infidelity is a prominent option," she paused. Nervous, she bit her lip gazing around the room hoping to attain enough integrity in her statements so that Miranda would listen, or at least localize the possibility of ideas not previously recognized by her own mind. "Like I said, I am sorry to automatically turn to adultery." Sighing, she starts again, "I just want what's best for you, and knowing you for as long as I have known you, I feel like I should be looking out for you, protecting you-"

"You don't need to protect me Josie!" Miranda snapped. Shocking them both. She regained her composure quickly. Adjusted her napkin on her lap, and took a drink from her glass. After setting her glass down, she reached for her fork and returned to her meal. Josie still startled, proceeded to follow her lead, and also returned to her dish. As for now, this conversational subject was most definitely over. But, Josie planned to help her friend figure out what's going on. She sure hoped she was wrong about Victor and his possible betrayal to Miranda. Finished with the silent treatment, she wanted to figure out a way to get her friend to loosen up and get out and enjoy herself. Miranda may not be ready to talk right now, but maybe if it was the right place, and time, Josie could get her to open up more about her situation.

"Uh, hey, what about tonight?"

Shaking her head, Miranda gave Josie a befuddled little squint with her eyes, "What about tonight?" "Weren't we going to get together and maybe have some drinks? I thought that's what the plan was. It's no big deal if you forgot."

"Oh, no, I didn't forget. Well, I forgot, but I did know I had something to do tonight. I guess that was it!" She said laughing. "What time did you want me to pick you up?"

"Ah...nine o'clock is good. Is that alright for you?"

"Yes ma'am, that's perfect for me. That will give me enough time to shower and relax. I have a few errands to do after this, so just being able to relax with my forever friend will be wonderful!"

They both smiled. Miranda was relieved that Josie didn't continue that dreaded conversation. Miranda didn't want to bring it up anyway, and thinking to herself again, I guess that I am being blatant about my feelings. I am never that obnoxious in my outer conveyance of emotions. Wow, getting older is not a good thing emotionally. She chuckled to herself, looked back at Josie and was thankful that they were friends. Josie really understood her so well. While Josie beamed back at Miranda's attempts to move on only to dessert, Josie had another plan scheming in her mind. Josie maintained that nine o'clock could not come fast enough.

*   *   *

Awakening to the sound of the doorbell, she picked up the clock next to her bathtub full of bubbles. Josie arrived promptly at nine o'clock. "Shit! I must have dozed off," thinking out loud. Scurrying out of the tub, Josie busted in to see a sopping wet Miranda wrestling to cover herself up with a towel. "I can't believe you aren't ready," Josie stated. She lifted her wrist to look at her watch, "It's nine-thirty. What are you doing?!"

"I'm so sorry Josie. I must have drifted off. I didn't do it intentionally, I promise. Give me fifteen minutes, I'll be ready," Miranda hurried around her room dropping shoes, and clasping articles of clothing, rushing around as not to keep her friend waiting longer than she already had.

Shouting from the foyer, a man's voice filled the house. Miranda and Josie looked at each other. Miranda thought Victor was supposed to be out of town until next week. Clasping her earring, she ran out of the bedroom, motioning for Josie to follow her. Josie gave an irritated sigh, and shadowed behind her.

"Hi baby! How are you?" She excitedly welcomed him. "Surprise! I'm home early!" He said, opening his arms wide for her.

"I know, I see that," she hesitated, " I thought you were going to be gone till next week? What happened?" "Oh, you know how it goes. Meetings get cancelled, so I got the next flight home, and here I am!" Looking around, he noticed that she was dressed up. "Are you going out?"

"Oh, well, yes, we had planned on it earlier in the week, and actually, were getting ready to head out right now." She felt as though she should cancel on her friend, but then thought about the times Victor was supposed to arrive home, and would always cancel on her. But, Josie, wouldn't mind, would she? "Well, I don't have to... You're home early! That's great!" Glancing at Josie, hoping she'd nod in agreement that changing plans would be an option; however, instead, she received a scowl. She could tell that Josie was extremely angry. Josie could not believe what she was hearing! Enraged, she stormed upstairs, "I'll get my purse Miranda."

Miranda knew Josie all too well. She was more than angry, she was irate. The fact that she was keeping herself together was something short of a miracle. If Miranda didn't do something about this situation immediately, she knew that her friendship with Josie would be strained indefinitely. "Look, honey, I already made plans with Josie. I love that you're home, and I really want to spend some needed time together; But..."

"I know. It's okay. You didn't expect me, and I can't just barge in on what you have going on. Tell you what," he scooped her up into his arms, holding her tightly, "you girls go out, and I'll just settle in tonight. Then, when you get home, maybe you and I can get in a little snuggle time. Sound good?"

"Sounds great! You're so wonderful!" They kissed each other as Josie returned down the stairs with her purse. She headed for the door, when Miranda stopped her.

"Hey! Where do you think you're going?"

"I believe you switched up our plans, did you not? I'm going home."

"Oh no you are not. We have some going out to do!"

Miranda said with a beaming smile, and crossed her arms.

Josie smiled back, "Let's go!"

Whew! That was a close one, Miranda thought. With all our issues between us, I am always surprised by Victor's awareness of others' feelings. What was she thinking earlier that he didn't love her anymore for? Silly Miranda, she thought to herself.

*   *   *

The lights were glittering about the room. The Top of the Hyatt at the Hyatt Hotel was dressed beautifully as usual. With glitterati every which way you looked, and fresh flowers atop the classic wooden cocktail tables surrounding the room. Dancing off the reflections of the strategically placed mirrors. Miranda ordered a dirty martini, sitting at their table gazing across the dance floor watching the people enjoy themselves. She watched a woman dance closely around a man, which she assumed was her husband, or hopefully something of the sort. She was dressed scantily clad with high-heeled thigh high boots. "Why on earth would a woman dress so provocatively," she murmured aloud to herself. Is that what it takes to get noticed by your man? Is that what I need to do to get my man's attention? Victor was so sweet earlier today about Josie and I going out, but usually he could care less. Who knows? One things for sure, I'm not planning on dressing like a hooker to get his attention. She started looking around the room trying to see where Josie went. She said she was going to the lady's room, but she hasn't yet returned. Hmm, she wondered to herself. Just as she finished taking a sip from her drink, a man stood before her.

"I said, hello." He said.

"Oh!" She abruptly sounded, "I'm sorry. I didn't see or hear you. Hi, um, I don't mean to be rude but I'm waiting for a friend."

"It's been a while, hasn't it?"

"I'm sorry" she squinted, trying to recall who this stranger might be. "Have we met before?"

He looked down, a little uncomfortable that she couldn't remember him, but never one to be defeated he decided to go forward with trying to jog her memory. "We met weeks ago, here at The Top of the Hyatt. I bought you a drink?" Shifting the weight of his body from one leg to the other, he chalked it up to not being remembered, and moved on with this. "My name is Johannes. Miranda, right?"

"You remembered my name. I would think you had since forgotten. I recall you now. You were dining with friends, or something?"

"Business meeting with colleagues."

"Oh. Alright." Pausing, Miranda felt her nerves overtake her normally gleaming personality. "Are you here with them again tonight?"

"Oh no. I'm actually taking some time off to relax." Something, I never do, he thought to himself. "How about yourself? You're here with your-"

"Friend. I'm here with my friend, Josie." She blurted out. Shaking her head shortly, with her eyes closed, and irritated with her own odd behavior, she spoke out again,

"Sorry. I'm just here with my friend, relaxing, doing the same as you I suppose." Hiding her left hand under the table that carries quite a large diamond ring on it.

"Where is she?"

"Who?" Who? What is wrong with me, "Josie," she laughed off, "She went to powder her nose, or something. But she's been gone for quite a while now."

"May I sit and keep you company? We wouldn't want any strange men coming along to pick up on you now, do we?"

Softening herself now, she smirked, and looked down at her glass, "No, I suppose we don't." With a pleasurable eye, she glanced at him, "At least you're an attractive strange man."

They scoffed together, and shared an entrancing stare. He flagged the waitress down and ordered himself a drink, and wanted to know more about her. He hasn't stopped thinking about her since they first met. What's she like? How does she take her tea? Does she even like tea? He wanted to know.

"Miranda, I have thought about you nonstop since we have first met. I thought we would never meet again. I almost gave up on it. Then I came in here tonight, hoping to see you, figuring that I wouldn't, but thought even if I didn't meet you again, just coming here would be reminiscent of it, and I would deal with that. I know we don't know each other in the least bit, but I want to know everything about you. I know this sounds strange, but I..." He was stumbling over his words, trying to find the right ones to say. He didn't want to scare her away, but then again he didn't want to miss this chance to just spill what he's feeling. "I have never felt this way about anyone."

"Look, Joh-"

"Don't say anything. Let me get this out. You may think I'm a 'whack-job' for even thinking of saying this considering we have only met one time; But, just give me a chance. Let me take you out for dinner, and get to know each other. Please."

"Jo-hawnes, right?"

He corrected her pronunciation, "Johannes."

"Sorry. Johannes. Look, I'm very flattered. I think you a very nice looking fellow, and any woman would be thrilled to have such an invitation, but-"

"Hey there my bestest, best best girlfriend in the whole wide world! Who's you're friend here?" Josie came barreling into Miranda's lap like a freight train. There was a drunken slur to many of her words, and Miranda could tell this was going to be even more difficult to get out of.

"Sooo, who's this? Hi! I'm Josie, Miranda's best friend. I have never seen you before?

"Hello, Josie." He raised one eyebrow to Miranda and raised his glass to her. "My name is Johannes. Your friend and I have met once before, I noticed her sitting here alone, and figured I'd help keep the riffraff's from trying to annoy her to take her to bed."

"Oh," Josie couldn't stop from laughing, " that would never happen."

"You can take care of yourself, huh?" He asked Miranda, winking and tipping his glass to her.

"Doesn't he know?" Josie giggled motioning her hands in Johannes direction.

"Don't I know what?" He responded.

"Ha! Miranda's mar-"

"Maker! I am also able to make pastries. I, on occasion spend all day baking pastries. Would you excuse us for a moment? It will just take one minute, excuse...uh, us."

Miranda abruptly and nervously grabs Josie, and start to drag her away from the table. "What are you doing?!" Miranda exclaimed.

"What are you talking about?" Josie says in a confused slurring of words.

"I didn't tell him I was married."

"Why not?" Suspicious, she exaggerates her facial expressions with shock, and then with great enthusiasm. "Have you been seeing someone outside your marriage Miss M.?"

Miranda looks across at Johannes, and gestures with her hand that they'll be back in a minute, and they head to the ladies restroom. "No. No, I have not been cheating on Victor. How dare you even consider such a thing! Josie, you know me better than that."

"Well, I was hoping that you were..." she looks up towards the ceiling, gives a roll of the eyes, and looks back at Miranda-as to irritate her-and continues on to say, "...since he's cheating on you."

"Enough. Victor is not cheating on me. He's a good man. Look, we're not getting into this right now. We're supposedly here to have a good time, do not tell Johannes I'm married, and let's just get on with the evening. Okay?" Miranda quiets herself as a woman exits a bathroom stall and glares at her in disgust. Miranda discreetly takes off her ring and lips it into her clutch.

"Why don't you want to tell this guy you're married?"

"Are you interested in him?"

After a long pause, Josie moves in closer to Miranda, and looks at her for an answer. Miranda rolls her eyes, and begins to storm out of the ladies room. She stops short of the door, turns back to Josie, and says "Johannes and I ran into one another once prior. I am not interested in him. We had things in common, and he was a nice gentleman. He happened to be here, and that's all there is to it. Let's go have fun, come on." She reaches for Josie's arm and they hook themselves together and gallop out the door.

"So, why aren't we telling him you're married?" Josie pops off to her one more time. Hoping to get an answer this time.

Miranda laughs at her instead and they head back to their table.

At a home, in the darkness, having an intimate conversation on the telephone, a dapper-looking man is trying to convince a woman to come over and spend some quality time together. He's sitting alone in his darkened study, and is trying to figure out how to get her to come by. "Baby girl, I really want to see you tonight."

"I know honey, but I just got home myself, and I'm winding down. I had such a hard day," she says to him, with a thickly coated Portuguese accent.

"That's why you need to stop in at my place. So, I can give you a nice rub down. Massaging all your tense muscles, and taking care of all your... needs." he tries to coerce her.

"Mmm, that does sound great. But, truly, I am just too exhausted. How did you get some free time?"

He pauses to think his reply through, then says, "Let's just say, I found a glitch in my schedule, and things just worked out. Worked out perfectly, for you and I, that is."

In a sultry, and sexy voice, she gives an approving declaration, "Well, my little millionaire, if it's worked out so lusciously, give me some time to get washed up, and beautiful for you, and come on over to my place instead. We can romp around some."

"It's a date," He says, then drops his arm down to put the receiver down.

"That Josie...She's quite a friend to you, isn't she?" Johannes quandaries.

"Yes, yes she is." Unsure of the nature of the question. She could feel that he was asking her and there would be more hereafter.

"What was it, that she was going to say before you and she ran off to the latrine?"

"What do you mean?"

"She had begun to say something about you, and in the midst of it, you trotted off with her hurriedly." Johannes responded with wonder.

"Oh, goodness, I haven't a clue. In fact, I don't even recall her speaking. A lot of drunken babbling, yes; But, nothing of a vital nature I'm sure." She said hoping to stop the arraignment.

"Would you like to dance Miss Miranda?"

Startled that a man would even take such an interest in her, she struggled with thoughts of infidelity. Fighting whether or not this was innocent behavior. Most certainly would be opposed if her husband was in this situation. Pausing, she bounced another thought in the opposite direction, although, she was lonely. Tired of being left to her own devices year in, and year out. "Sure! Let's go."

"Ok then," he stood reaching for her hand, and they moved to the center of the dance floor. Miranda was having such a grand time, but the time itself was of no issue to her. If she could stay here forever, that would be alright with her. Johannes was so handsome, and such a gentleman, she had forgotten what it was like to feel a bit alive. Over the DJ's microphone she could hear him announcing the last song of the evening was being set to play. As she heard that, Johannes moved in closer to her, grasping his arm around her waist, and clutching her hand in his. Bumped up against his body, all she could think about was this animalistic inclination to ravish him and let him do as he damn well pleased to her!

He could smell the faintness of lavender from her hair. Sweat glistening off of her neck from dancing with him. He hadn't had such a better time with anyone in his entire life. He pulled her even closer; so close that he could feel her heart beating fast against his. He took in a deep breath, looked into her eyes. With his hand lifting her chin, she gazed back at him.

Miranda was thinking so many things at one time. I'm married. I'm married. I'm married, she kept telling herself. What am I supposed to do here? I am totally into this guy, and I know I shouldn't be, but I am, and what about my husband? Oh God, what am I going to do?

And in that moment, he leaned into her, kissing her, gently, yet full of something she couldn't even explain. She felt lost in her thoughts, felt confused by what was happening. Her heart was racing; her body was pulsating. And then...and then she felt herself enjoying this moment in time. For once she felt joy, pure joy. She felt wanted. This man wanted her, she had no clue who he was, or really where he came from, but he wanted her. The room stood still between them. As still as she felt the outside world could only have been, with an intrusive bounce Josie impeded her presence.

"Ow!" Miranda shouted, rubbing her forehead. Upon impact, Josie managed to collide both Miranda, and Johannes head to head.

Laughing, "Sorry, I was just noticing the time girl! We gotta get out of here. Johannes it was great meeting you and your British accent." After a short pause, and a observing sly gazes between the two of them, she said slurring, "Hey Johannes! Aren't ya going to ask Miranda for her number. You all met once before did you not?"

Laughing at Josie, Johannes eyes Miranda and says to her, "She's right. I'm not letting you get away this time without a phone number. May I have it?"

Her heart was racing, and her thoughts were fighting. Her pounding heart was screaming and jumping at the 'yes' she so wanted to reply; But, her thoughts were griping, and moaning over the solid facts that entailed her personal life.

"Hell with it!" Josie blathered. "Here, this is her cell phone. She does a lot of volunteer and deals with a lot of old people with her, old maid's clubs. Call her, stalk her, do whatever you gotta do; but, for now we're out of here. Smooches!" She finished up writing down Miranda's number, and handed him the napkin on which she wrote, and blew him a kiss while grabbing for her friend for life.

"Look Miss Thang, I may be a little drunk; Although, not blind. That man was kissing you!" Josie lowered her volume, and closed in on Miranda's ear, "You have a husband."

"No kidding Josie. Why did you give him my number?"

"I was trying to get us out of here. When I saw you guys kissing, I was stunned... And proud at the same time. It was a very strange moment for me." Josie muttered.

"Josie. You said go for it! Live it up! Blah, blah, whatever else, and now you're off-kilter over my lip-locking?!" She started getting upset. She felt so enlivened, so airy, and now it was all going to shit because Josie was getting all moralistic on her. What the hell was going on here?

"Honey. I said go for it, yes. I just meant, let's get out and let loose. Dance it up, have a few drinks, take in a few laughs. Get the stress of things off your head. I didn't say go make out with Dr. Hunk!"

After a long pause, they sat in the car and just burst out laughing. "Dr. Hunk." Miranda repeated back to her while rolling her eyes. Miranda started the car, and headed home. "You can stay at my house tonight."

"Ok." Giggling, Josie hardly containing herself replied, "Besides, I may have had one drink too many."

"No? You don't say..." Miranda teased, laughing and rolling her eyes.

4

Chapter Four

"How's that Lockon account coming along? Are there any new developments?" Quarried Johannes.

"Well," started Gary, "It appears as though we have hit a snag."

"How so?" This worried Johannes because everything was riding on this account. The firm had lost some investors recently due to some bad business dealings he had encountered with a colleague. Mark Bevent had met in their fraternity in college. They became somewhat close. He, Gary, and Johannes would run around being reckless with women, with panty raids and alcoholic escapades. Out of the three of them, Mark was the most mischievous, the most outlandish. After college they went their separate ways for quite some time and ran into Mark again when he first moved himself to San Diego. Johannes offered Mark a job in doing some accounting work for his then new business for which Johannes new would be successful one day. They worked well together and business had been booming. He had entrusted Mark Bevent with a few of the ledgers relating to some very important investors, Ledgers that hadn't Johannes not been so busy with other accounts would had normally handled himself-and unbeknownst to him, Mark had been laundering funds to himself overseas. After some suspicious behavior, Johannes began to investigate his own employees. When he received an anonymous tip that he should check out his own long time buddy, he painfully turned Mark's name over for thorough investigation as well. It turned out that Mark was the culprit, and while the matter was resolved and Mark was sentenced appropriately; the blemish it had left on Johannes' firm tarnished his reputation. The news crews were at his doorstep on a daily basis during that period, and had a field day with titles enticing the public to read: 'foreign businessman under siege in our San Diego.' Even with the good business dealings he had spent so long to build, the media went gaga over it. And the bad press was still affecting him from time to time.

Taking in a deep breath, Gary started slowly, "It seems as though someone has sent an anonymous letter detailing the gossip about those companies involved with our firm, and..."

Johannes felt a surge of rage run through him. He had worked too damn hard for it all to fall apart because of some nobody gallivanting a tirade about town out to ruin good people's names! "Mark Bevent." The word's left his lips with such anger, and hatred he could not believe this guy was still out to ruin him. Johannes started pacing the room, his arms crossed, and his face scorn. "We're going to stop this asshole for good." He stopped and pointed at Gary.

"Wh-What are we going to do? We can't be sure it's even him."

"I don't know yet, but Mark Bevent is going to wish he was never born." Johannes said with surety.

The intercom beeped and Gary reached over to see who was on the line.

"Uh, Mr. Johannes, sir," his secretary called, "you have a visitor from Lockon Properties. Are you available?"

"Sure. Sure. Let them in," he responded. "Alright, whatever we do, keep what we have just discovered under wraps. I don't want this to blow the deal."

"Johannes, what about all thi-"

"Just keep your mouth shut Gary," He stated firmly.

The door opens, and without surprise it was Gayle. "Hello gentleman. Thanks for seeing me without an appointment, I had some urgent issues to address on this proposal and I wanted to get it done before I had to fly out of here this afternoon. How are we this morning?"

Gary and Johannes exchange glances, and offer a seat to Gayle. "Things are relative on this end. And to what do we owe this pleasure?" Johannes questioned.

"I just wanted to go over pages six, twelve, and nineteen of these notes. On page six, section eight, paragraph three, it seems to be incongruent with page twelve, paragraph one. Also, on page nineteen Lockon Properties shows disapproval with the percentage at which you would gain profit. Not much pleasure I'm afraid....at least, not this time Johannes." Gale winked at him, adding a wry smile.

Gary looked at Johannes in disbelief, opening his mouth to say something out of shock. Johannes eyed him and cut him off before he could even begin to speak, Johannes calls to the secretary to take notes. In regards to page six, section eight, paragraph three, and page twelve, paragraph one. The incongruence lies only if a breach comes into acceleration. Page nineteen carries a varied percentage based upon performance among my firm and yours. The percentage at which

Oxenburg Investment Enterprises gains profit is manipulated by overhead accumulated, but not limited to, execution of detailed matters included in the manifest-page two, section eleven, paragraph five, and subparagraphs 'j' and 'k'- as well as any future acquired profit gained by Lockon Properties due to O.I.E.'s direct dealings in the present." He releases the intercom, and raises his eyes in serious tone to her, "Anything else Ms. Lockharte?"

"If I could just acquire a copy of the minutes stated here today, that would be appreciated. I will be back with another query should there need be a week or so from today."

"Thank you Ms. Lockharte, send Mr. Lockon my best."

She rises from her seat, shakes hands, and heads for the door, "I'll do that Johannes. And, as I told you before when we last met, we're on a first name basis now. There's hardly any room to be proper now, don't you think?" She snickered, and nodded her head to Gary, "Mr. Solden..."

*   *   *

Seated in a sunny veranda, Miranda sips her tea while intrigued by her reading. Her husband sits across from the table his attention intensely directed to his morning paper. She takes a moment to absorb her surroundings. A brightly colored blue sky, with the whitest and fluffiest of clouds. Her wicker-made furniture, dipped in a silky pearl. She ran her fingers across the interwoven material, and across the glass topped with an array of beautiful flowers arranged magnificently. She admired the perfectly cut green grass that swept across the vast lawn, which was met at all corners with courageous blooms that seemed to just pop out and grab your attention no matter where you stood.

"What are your plans today dear?" Victor asked.

"Oh, nothing really. I thought I would dawdle into town today, and visit the shops. I was eyeing such a stunning chapeau that would be remarkable for times such as these. How about yourself?"

"I'm going to head into the city. There's a few deals I need to keep an eye on because of their sensitivity with content. I have to keep that rolling in, or no more chapeau's for you missy." Victor joked.

"Will you be home late again?" She asked innocently.

"More than likely," he calmly said, "you know how it goes my dear."

"Yes. Yes, I know." She said sadly into his eyes. He looked back at his paper, and she took another sip from her cup, and returned to her novel.

Before she could get settled in, Rose, the caretaker of the property walked up with phone in hand, and reported to Victor's ear who must've been on the line. He nodded at Miranda, thanked Rose, and headed off into the house. Miranda couldn't help but wonder what with the secrecy. He never let her in on what his business dealings really entailed. All she knew was that he would go into the city, come home, and return to the city and so on. She would-on occasion-ask what it was he would do all day and sometimes night in the city; But he would grunt a few confusing explanations and disappear out of the room. This would disturb her only for a while, then she would rationalize that there's nothing to worry about, and if he didn't want to be with her, he would have divorced her by now. Or maybe, she thought, because I don't really dig my heels into him about things, that's exactly what he wanted from a wife. Someone that wouldn't make waves, wouldn't dare be suspicious, just go with what's expected.

That was exactly who Miranda was. Someone who would never make a mountain out of a molehill. Someone who would stand idly by and watch life pass her. And, while all was progressing, and becoming something great, she would always be Victor Setes' wife, a woman that was extremely involved in her community, a socialite with an endearing heart for the poor. She sat just staring into space, and lost in her thoughts of all she had known, might just be a big lie. Was Josie right to tell me that Victor doesn't love me? That he just loves that I stay in the lines of what's expected of me? How could watching Victor and Rose interact in such an odd way have gotten me to reach for answers on who I'm supposed to be? She sighed, shook her head, and tossed the rambling thoughts aside. She got up from her chair and walked inside. Victor was rushing around grabbing his briefcase, and keys.

"Well, gotta go. There's some sort of crisis at one of the branches, and I need to take care of things. I'll see you later."

She leaned toward him in hopes of getting any type of affection from him, and to her dismay, she as usual received nothing. She sighed, and went upstairs.

*   *   *

Miranda finishes her bathing routine, and walks into the bedroom in her robe, and the phone rings. "Hello?"

"Hey, it's Josie! How did it go with that sexy man from the bar....Joo-haaaanes?"

Miranda laughs, "You just won't quit will you?"

"Hey, I've got an unhappily married friend whom says she's happily married, but gets hit on by a beautiful man that no woman can resist....it's a regular soap opera I tell ya!" After a short pause, "so?"

"So, what?"

"So, did you call him yet? Come on, I have no life here, none man, I need some excitement, and you got it sister! So, out with it already, spill it!"

Miranda sighs, and displays a slight smirk to herself, "No. I didn't-"

"What?!"

"I didn't ca-"

"I can't believe it!" Josie screams, overreacting, "Here you are with Mr. Perfect and you are spending the day looking for who knows what, or probably nothing, and you aren't calling him! He's... He's.."

"He's my problem. I am not going to-"

"Problem?! He's no problem Miranda! He's the Godsend to all women and he wants you!"

"Like I was trying to say, I'm not going to stalk him, or be overly anxious. I'm sure women act like that all the time towards him. You would scare him away," giggling at Josie's rash behavior.

"Maybe I would, but damn it all to hell if I didn't take that chance. He has everything that Victor can give you, but I guarantee more!"

"You don't know anything about him Josie."

"I looked him up. After we got home, I wrote his name down. Since I knew I wouldn't remember it because I was so, uh...well, tipsy."

Miranda let out an obnoxious level of gaiety. "Josie, you were drunk!"

"Anyway, however you want to read it, I did write his name down and looked him up. He gave millions to charities over the years, he's a transplant from England. He came to America to "live the American dream", and even though his family in Europe are extremely well comforted, he came here on his own and is a made man. Besides, on top of all that, he probably lays the pipe pretty good in bed-"

"Josie!" Miranda was never shocked by Josie's outbursts but oddly this one caught her off-guard. Mostly because she had so many deviant thoughts lately over this... Johannes, that she wasn't thinking straight. She wondered why he was interested in her. She was older than him, but certainly not enough to be categorized the cradle-robbing type. "Oh God, but he was handsome," she thought to herself. She had never felt that way about Victor. He was the epitome of what her parents wanted for her, and that's what she did. She always did what others wanted of her. Maybe it was time for her to make a change? Maybe I need to shake things up?

"Listen Josie, even if I did call him, what would I say? What would I do? Oh, Hi there! I met you at a bar, and now this slut wants a piece..." She shook her head, but knew that Josie would have an answer.

"Miranda, you do want to call him, don't you?"

"Josie, just, what would I say?"

Josie laughed with cockiness, "I knew it! Alright," she paused, "I don't know."

"What?" Miranda stated in shock.

"Well, I mean, usually when a man hit on you in a bar it's to get some ass. But he didn't seem like he wanted you like that. I saw how he kissed you, and-"

"You saw that! Oh my God, Josie I. It wasn't-"

"Slow down. It's alright. I know I have been giving you a hard time; but, seriously, you know me! I'm the last person to judge you girl, so just relax. I think the way he kissed you was more... Passionate, not sexual."

Miranda thought her comments through for a while.

"Not that he doesn't want you sexually," she blurted quickly. "But you know what I mean."

"Yeah, I know what you mean.. But, what do you I say to him now?" She felt so much angst in this.

"Hmm. I think you should just call him up, and say a simple hello."

"Ok. Hello. That should work."

"Then, after you say that, ask him when you two can bump like bunnies!" Josie's laughter was so loud it distorted the phone's reception.

"Thanks, Josie," Miranda rolled her eyes.

"I gotta go," still laughing so hard she could barely speak.

"Bye." They both hang up, and Miranda is left to herself agonizing what it is she is going to say. What if he doesn't even remember me now?

What if he is just looking for a one night stand? I don't want to become a part of that. But then again, something with no strings-No. Not my style. Definitely not an option. She spends a few minutes getting some tea, sitting back in the chair, and reaching for the number. She eyes it for a long duration, and decidedly picks up the phone. And on the other end she hears a voice.

"Hello."

5

Chapter Five

Inside the grand ballroom which overlooked the Pacific Ocean was fantastic. The ceilings were draped with Swarovski chandeliers, ribbons of sheer satin fabrics in deep colors of purples, oranges and reds. The tabletops were set with beautifully arranged hydrangeas in deep blue, with orange tulips peeking out, and hints of thin, deep green lengthy grass and golden bamboo. Miranda had been to many of these types of events, either through her charity balls, or many of Victor's business engagements, and the yearly plethora of invites that routinely come to their doorstep for which she has been elected to decide which are more important requiring their attendance.

"Wow Victor, this year you really went all out for your employees," Miranda snuggled in closer to him, reaching her arm through his. Victor pulled away as he noticed some business associates approaching. Left to herself, Miranda decided to retreat to the ladies room to powder her nose.

She stared at herself in the mirror holding back any emotion that would conjure up tears. What girl wants to ruin her makeup? She couldn't help but think to herself why Victor had been so distant. He had been elusive all evening, and when she had tried to engage him with conversation or spend a little couple time when he'd had a minute, he simply had cast her aside claiming he had another prospect to propose. "We've been distant before," she thought. And usually with these types or soirees, he's very focused on how he presents his image to possible contacts and closing contracts. But, the past couple months, it's almost as if she believed they've been pulled apart by something big. "I just know he maybe cheating on me. No, no. I'm thinking like Josie now. He would never do that to me. He loves me. He would want a divorce if he wanted to see another woman." As she was in her thoughts a woman approached next to her in the mirror.

"Fabulous party, don't you think?" The woman asked.

"Yes. They sure do know how to throw them."

"My fiancé is the man responsible for this gala," she stated the fact, and as she spoke Miranda's gaze became more of a shock. Continuing on in her Portuguese accent, "He loves to go big! Just look at my engagement ring."

Miranda glanced at it, and returned to the mirror to apply some lipstick. Who was she talking about? Victor is the one who set this whole thing up. Was this the woman Victor is sleeping with? Oh my God, it couldn't be. She tried to focus and remain intact. "So, when's the wedding date?"

"Early spring of next year. He has some loose ends he needs to tie up and that won't be able to finish until then."

"Well, that's just wonderful dear. What's your lucky groom's name?"

"Vic. He's so wonderful, but I can't tell you his whole name because his wife might be here. I've never met her, and he says nice things about her, but truly, the sooner he dumps her, the sooner I can reap my benefits, you know what I mean." she was snorting and laughing, shrugging her shoulders, and happily put her cosmetics back into her glamorous bag that Miranda was sure 'Vic' bought for her. She could feel her whole body tensing up with anger, and fear, and... Well, I don't know what else, but I did want to punch this broad.

As the hussy left the bathroom, I immediately dialed Josie. I looked under the stalls and throughout the bathroom to make sure that no one else was in there.

"Hello?"

"Oh thank God you answered Josie! You're not going to believe what, I mean who I just ran into. You were right. You were right all along! I can't believe what a fool I was. Oh dear, Josie, what do I do?" Miranda was intensely whispering trying not to be heard by anyone, not even if that anyone was on the other side of the bathroom door passing by, and just happened to hear a hysterical woman crying over a newfound revelation.

"Miranda? Ok, honey, you need to slow down. I can't make sense of anything your saying. What was I right about? Who? Start slowly."

"Ok." Breathing heavily, and trying to relax. She started, "Victor and I are here at the company extravaganza. He is behaving as usual, ignoring me, pushing me aside. You know."
"ah-hum," Josie knows something is coming, and its bad. Miranda is never this anxious.

"So, I go to the restroom to powder up and a woman comes and stands next to me. She starts talking to me, and realize I'm already in a bad mood since Victor has cast me aside all evening, and this woman show me her engagement ring to a guy that's married. His name is Vic."

"Oh my God Miranda, I didn't want--you're sure she was talking about your Victor?" She asked with genuine concern.

"Josie, she said to me she was whispering because his wife was here, and not to say anything. And, that her 'fiancé' was the one who put this whole party together. Who else could she possibly be talking about?" There was a long pause. She looked around the ladies room again making sure no one was there. "How could I not see this coming? I have been such a good wife to him."

"Miranda. Wait there. I am on my way. Don't act like you know ok? Just pretend everything is fine."

"No, I don't need you coming to rescue me."

"I'm not coming to rescue you, my best gal pal, I'm coming to stir up some trouble!" And with that she hung up the phone, without giving Miranda the chance to respond.

Miranda grabbed some tissue to dry her eyes. Glanced at her reflection one last time, took a deep breath, and with every ounce of pride she had left, she exited gracefully. As she came around the beautifully decorated celebration, she saw Victor talking to a naturally tanned, dark-haired woman. As she got closer she could see that it was the same woman from the stall. As quickly as she realized, she ducked behind a large artifact bumping it. As it wobbled she attempted to steady it, hoping it would not drop and shatter. The last thing she needed was to have any attention brought to her tonight. The wobbling stopped, and she straightened the wrinkles in her silk dress. As she looked back up she found herself looking into the face of a beautiful man directly in front of her.

"Good thing I was around to stop you from breaking things."

"What are you doing here?" Slightly surprised, she quickly retracted, "I'm sorry. That was rude."

"And after the grand conversation we had the other evening, I thought for sure I had caught your attention."

She smirked, "I know." Glancing around the room, making sure no one saw her talking to Johannes. "Are you an acquaintance of the host?"

"I am actually working on a project with the host. He is a silent partner in an endeavor my company is forging. What brings you here?"

"Oh, I'm... I do a lot of charity work, and some of the proceeds go to a few, chosen particular charities funded through my non-profit." Quickly realizing her wedding ring was in plain sight, and hid it behind her.

"That's right, Kid DreamZ, correct?"

"Good memory." Again, Miranda was lost in his eyes, and her heart was palpitating. Oh how she yearned for him to draw her close again. To feel her body against his.

"Well, well, well. I thought we'd never see you again, and of all places.. Here you are!" Josie abruptly interjected. "Miranda, I got here as fast as I could; But, I see you have everything under control here, so I will just get out of your way."

"No, no." Miranda gave her a glare. "Uh, Johannes, you remember Josie?"

"How could I forget." He nodded, and turned back to Miranda. "Is there some sort of emergency?"

"What?" Miranda choked.

"Uh, no," Josie blurted. Every thing's fine. Wardrobe malfunction-will you excuse us?" She grabbed Miranda's hand and they headed anywhere away from Johannes.

"Well, that explains why you were hiding behind the plants." He laughed.

"Ha.. Ha, yeah, right." So embarrassed, she and Josie secluded themselves somewhere to talk. "I can't believe this is happening. Look at me, trying to act like Janet Jackson at the Super bowl..." Putting up a finger to Johannes, "...Ah, we'll be back!"

"Did you invite him here?"
"Uh, nooo. I ran into him, after I ran into the statue, almost knocking it over while I was trying to hide from Victor talking to that same woman I talked to in the bathroom."

"It just keeps getting better and better!" Josie was so excited. This made Miranda nervous.

"What do I do? Now Johannes is here, and I am going to have to avoid him. If I'm seen with him it could ruin my whole reputation."

"Look, I think we're getting ahead of ourselves here. No one knows you know him except me. Okay? So, let's just focus on the first problem. You're sure he's cheating with that girl you saw him with?"

"Yes. You know when you talk to someone, and you have had sex with them? That sort of comfort-ability, that body language? I could just tell. And, she was too young to afford such a lavish engagement ring, and she said her fiancée's name was 'Vic', he's the one throwing this bash, and on top of it, she said he was married. So, uh, hello? I'm completely positive that he's having an affair with this woman."

"I know exactly what to do. Let's go."

"What are we going to do?"

"Never mind. Just be you, and I'll take care of this tramp. And Victor will be none the wiser."

Later in the evening when the dinner had completed the honors and awards were to be handed out, and everyone who was the richest would do some motivational speaking. Always boring. Josie and I sat at our table, and she tapped me.
"Which one is it?"
"Huh?"
"Which slut is it?"
Shaking my head, I inconspicuously eyed the room until I spotted her. "There she is. She wearing a Gautlier gown, black."

"He has her dressed kindly now doesn't't he?" Josie whispered glancing around the room. Spotting her she shrieks a little loudly, "What?! Is she fifteen?" Josie was never one to hold her tongue.

They glared at her until she noticed them, and quickly making sure that Victor wasn't paying any mind, both Josie and Miranda waved at this other woman. The other woman smiled, and realizing with a stupefying look on her face, that Miranda was the same woman in the bathroom, and the same woman sitting next to-her fiancé! The other woman was floored and avoided eye contact and physical contact from Miranda, and Victor for the rest of the evening.

"Problem solved." Josie proudly acknowledged.
"How do you figure? They're still going to talk, or worse have sex."

"Probably so; However, now she knows, that you know. And not only you, but me too. Which means now she is going to run to Victor and look like a maniac? I guarantee he isn't going to acknowledge that you might know what's going on." Continuing to whisper, as Victor rose up from his seat to wave to everyone-as he was spoken about how great he was by another person- "He's too much of an ego-maniac to quit you. He is going to hang on to both of you until it unravels at his feet." Just as she finished, Johannes was walking up to the podium. "Now there's someone you need to be with." Miranda smiled at her and turned her attention to Johannes.

"Ladies and gentleman. Miraculous things occur when great men are able to get together and create. I thank you all for coming, and allowing a chance for Kid Dreams to help more underprivileged children here in our city, and nationwide. A round of applause for Miranda Setes. As you all know, I am a big supporter of charity. My enterprise has given more than its fair share to different contributions. And to Victor Setes, the man of the evening!" He raised his glass, and in doing so, he was cognizant of the fact that Miranda and Victor were... married? He stalled his thoughts for a moment, and made eye contact with Miranda. She gave an approving look confirming his comprehension. "Uh, as I was saying, Victor, the man of the evening, let's keep filling up our pockets, so that we can be.. Richer!" Everyone applauded in roaring laughter, "And to your family, Victor, you're a lucky man!"

*   *   *

"Wow. Did you see the way he looked at you when he gave his speech?" Josie muttered.

"Look, I can't worry about him now, we have to focus on-"

"Good evening Josie, Miranda didn't tell me you were coming tonight?" Just as Miranda had begun, Victor came into view. "You know my dear, this was supposed to be for you and I to spend together."

"Maybe she wouldn't have to invite me along if you weren't busy cavorting with-" Miranda nudged her.

"Uh, Victor, I invited Josie along because you had been busy working the room. It's alright, we can spend time later when we get home. I hope it isn't a bother that I invited her."

"Of course not. But, after the party, I need to get to the office and take care of some things. Come Monday, there are a lot of contracts that will need to be finished, and I don't want any unlikely surprises." He toasted his glass to an associate across the room. He kissed Miranda on the cheek and scurried along.

"I guess we're not spending time together tonight." Miranda muttered under her breath, "Not that we have thus far tonight anyhow."

"Did you think you would?" A stern voice came from behind me.

"Hello Johannes!" Josie shouted in excitement. She turned to me and under her breath quickly, "This is your chance. Take it girl." And Josie turned to Johannes, "Well, it was lovely seeing your handsome face again, but I think I'm going to leave you two kids alone and find myself a sugar daddy! Smooches!"

As Miranda watched Josie throttle off, she let out a giggle. "Ah, that girl. She can always see opportunity."

"I see opportunity." He said matter-of-factly. "In fact, when we met, I saw you from across the room. And decided in that moment, I had to meet you. Then in doing so, I was so insanely nervous, I just was beside myself. Followed by a long conversation which had me enamored, and now, again, I see you from across the room..." Oh no, Miranda thought. Don't say it out loud. "With your husband."

"Wait, I can explain-"

"No. No need. But, I will let you in on a little secret."

Afraid of what she's about to hear, she gets the courage to meekly sputter, "What's that?"

"Well, let's put it this way, that girl you saw him talking to earlier?"

"You saw them talking together too?"

"Yes."

"So they are?"

"Yes."

"Yes," In shock, Miranda motions to find her a seat. Johannes gets her safely to a chair, and she continues in a whisper, "I knew it. I mean, I thought I knew, but when I 'thought' I knew, I really did already...know."

"I'm sorry. Believe me, I am not happy that I am the one to confirm it, but he introduced her to me once before, and I assumed they were-"

"Stop. What?!"

"He's been spotted with her at many social gatherings. So, it was quite a shock to me watching him toast to you as his wife, and I... I didn't know Miranda." There was a shared moment of silence between them. "I know you may believe that I want nothing more than to get you into bed. But honestly, even if you had told me you were married, I would have pursued you. I have never felt this way about someone."

"Look, Johannes, I don't know what to say. Right now, I cannot think of us as anything. I just found out by a man I hardly know that my husband has been seeing another woman for a while now, and on top of that, earlier the woman herself relieved this information to me herself."

"Are you kidding?" He asked puzzled.

"No. I wish I was. She obviously didn't know I was Victor's wife. Although, she knows now." She giggled a bit. "I saw them talking earlier this evening, so later, I went to the ladies' room for privacy, then she told me, (or rather vomited) that information on me-not realizing I was the wife, and I called Josie. That's why Josie's here. I just can't believe this. I really don't know why I trusted him so much!"

"Oh, I just figured Josie was attached to your hip." Johannes said jokingly.

As apparent as the joke did not come across, Miranda replied, "Would you drive me home? I just don't feel like," she looked up at him with the most intense sadness in her eyes. As her eyes welled up with tears, she forced them back and attempted to keep her composure as she continued, "Uh, would you mind Johannes?"

"No. Not at all."

As they were leaving, Johannes had looked around to make sure no one took notice of them together. Not that it would have mattered. In fact, it would have been better because most of her acquaintances and his would be happy that she was finally getting something she deserved out of her relationship with Victor. It made Johannes so angry that Victor would mistreat such a beautiful creature. As they made their way down the stairs, Josie came running up.

"Hey guys! Are you leaving?"

Miranda and Johannes turned back towards her. Josie saw how unhappy Miranda was, and nodded. She also raised her glass to them in approval.

As they pulled up to Miranda's home, Johannes walked around the car to open her passenger side door. Groggily, she exited the vehicle with the help of his strong, masculine hands. They walked to the door, and she unlocked it, letting herself in. As she stepped over the threshold, she turned to him letting the door open itself the rest of the way, "Thank you so much Johannes. I am so sorry you had to find out I was married this way. Please understand, I wanted to tell you but-"

He put his fingers to her lips, "Shh. Listen. I don't know what it is about you, but it's you. I want you. I will wait for you. I know we don't know each other hardly at all," and as he was speaking, she felt this profound feeling overcome her and she leaned towards him. Moving his hands from her face to her bosom. He stopped what he was saying, "Don't think this is why I said I'd bring you home."

"Shh... I'll worry about the details tomorrow." She looked into his eyes, and as they embraced, they passionately kissed. With all electricity between them, as they kissed, he backed her into the house, shutting the door behind him. She dragged him by his luscious lips until she could back up no more. Laying her against the steps of the stairs, she eyed him, opening her legs to receive him.

He came in close, kneeling in front of her body, sliding her silky evening gown up over her legs, exposing their shapeliness. He ran his hands up her thighs squeezing them, opening them to invite him closer and he whispered, "Are you sure you want to do this?"

"I'm sure." She nodded, letting her hair down. She had never felt such passion from a man before. He kissed along her ear, down her neck.

He unleashed the top-side of her gown exposing her plump breasts. He ripped his shirt off, causing buttons to fly across the room. Lowering himself, he suckled each of her breasts enlightening her to let out a soft, well deserved moan. She reached one of her arms up to grab the banister, and the other grabbing for his pants. "Take them off," she whispered excitedly. As he hurriedly took them off, she moved her elegant panties to the side of her sweetness. Showing him that he is more than welcome to come taste her.

He came in close to her again, and what she thought was going to be something to rise her emotions again, was really, "Is Victor coming home after the party?"

Quickly, her thoughts raced, her heart palpitated with worry. Why would he bring his name up now? It's a little late to be thinking about-oh, I don't know-my husband! And before she could open her mouth to speak, he looked her endearingly in her eyes, and entered her with his manhood. As he did this, she let out such a heavy breath, a moan of equal proportions came thereafter. She tilted her head back, and screamed in delight as he pushed himself deep inside her, back and forth, rising her temperature. He licked up her neck, grasping her waist to keep their bodies in sexual synchronized rhythm.

"Look at me." He stated in pleasurable grandeur.

As she looked at him, his breath collided with hers, and he kissed her, swallowing her like the soft peach he believed she was, he pulled his head back, moaning, and came in close again. This time whispering in her ear, "This is all yours baby. I will never do you wrong. We deserve each other," and as he spoke those words to her, they came together. Shrieking in pure unadulterated delight.

Breathing heavily, they pulled themselves off the staircase and Johannes, stumbling over his words said, "I am-I had no intention of-"

"Stop." Miranda still trying to find her breath. "We're alone tonight," tickling his chest, "and, Victor won't be here. He said he'd be downtown tying up loose ends, blah, blah, blah. Which, we now know is a lie."

"What are you saying?" He asked, picking her up, and taking her up the stairs to her bedroom.

Laughing she says, "I'm saying," As she kissed him underneath his jaw line, and again on his neck, "I want you here with me." And she kissed him once more just under his ear, giving it a light nip with her teeth.

He gently lay her on her African-orange colored Egyptian cotton sheets. With such a ridiculous thread count, that only the touch and feel of them is required to materialize the unique, almost orgasmic suppleness usually associated with this type of sheet. He removed the rest of her clothing, and began to caress her velvety smooth skin...

*   *   *

Then next morning, Miranda awoke to the sight of Johannes sound asleep. She placed stray strands of hair to the side of his face, to study his features. He opened his eyes to her watching him, and he gave a sincere smile. He leaned over and kissed her protruding lips, "Would you like to go out to breakfast?"

Returning his gaze, she responded with a smile, "Johannes, I would love to, but I don't think it would be a good idea."

Johannes started to bustle his belongings together, and began to get ready to leave. Miranda just looked down to the bed, and then looked back at him, "I just think we run the risk of getting caught. He knows my schedule-"

"Miranda. I understand your situation. Now understand this. Victor doesn't care about you. Look around you. It's 11:00 am, and he hasn't shown up, he hasn't called, he isn't here." Raising his voice slightly,

"I want to be with you, and only you. You are a great woman, and the sooner you realize that, the sooner you can be available to me."

"Maybe he hasn't shown up here at home, or called. But the fact of the matter is, I am married to him. I can't just cast aside eighteen years of marriage. There's too much to lose."

"Too much to lose? Too much to lose." Johannes nodded his head and walked straight towards the exit. He turned back before leaving and said, "You've already lost Miranda."

6

Chapter Six

Miranda sat gazing out her window longing to feel his touch once more. Embracing the warmth of his breath against hers. She had felt things she hadn't felt in years with this man. She couldn't get his scent off of her. She realized she'd made a mistake with Johannes. Johannes was a strapping man with a strong jaw line, and distinguished features. He was beautifully wrapped within the family appearances and business dealings he upheld. Yet, no matter how much she wished she could take back the moments that are now capturing her every thought and memory, she couldn't vanquish how much joy and excitement he had brought to her life.

"I haven't heard from him in weeks Josie."

"What did you expect? You basically told him forget about anything we just did, move along, and I'll call you when I'm good and ready."

"That's not what I meant. I just wanted him to understand that we made a mistake doing what we did."

With caution, and tremendous care, Josie touched Miranda's hand with concern and said, "Forget for one moment that you're married, forget about your social status, and what other people think. How did Johannes make *you* feel Miranda?"

"I-I can't answer that Josie."

"Bullshit! And the truth is that he made you feel like you've never felt before! He saw in you, and you felt it in you. No pun intended." Josie giggled.

Sighing, "So, what do I do?"

"You go get him girl!"

Scratching her head, and deep in concentration, "How do you propose I do that? Look, it's just not that easy Josie. Weeks have passed by, we haven't spoken, and things have gone on as they were meant to be. We had one great night together, and I can be thankful for that if nothing else. Now just let it go."

"Ok. Fine." Irritated, she stood up, "That's just beautiful Miranda. You just let the love of your life slip through your fingers. Continue on in misery. Because in reality, your husband is going to leave you for that other woman, and Johannes will be long gone too. At least you have rationalized it for yourself though."

"Meaning what?"

"Meaning," She started to leave, grabbing for her handbag, and turned back to drop an envelope on the table, "That Johannes was just some guy that fulfilled an evening of something you will never get again." And with that, she left flipping open her cell phone.

*   *   *

Miranda decided that some fresh air at this point would be delightful. There was just too much tension on her head, and she needed to clear her mind. She took a drive and found herself downtown in front of the Oxenburg Investment Enterprises building. What was she thinking she would accomplish by being here? He basically said he loved me without actually spilling those words out. She calculated as she took each step up to the elevator. As she rode up the elevator, she found her nerves strangling her insight. *What am I doing here? Have I completely lost my mind? No, no. Stay calm Miranda.* She checked her appearance in the reflective metal of the doors. As the elevator announced the top floor has arrived, she took a deep breath and stepped out into the Lobby. She was greeted by an upbeat and youthful secretary.

"Who are you here for?"

"I'm, uh," she cleared her throat, "I'm here to see Johannes. Johannes Oxenburg Please." She straightened up as she spoke the last word.

"And, you are?" She asked rather rudely.

"I'm a friend. Could you just let him know that Miranda is here? I just was in the neighborhood and-"

"Well, well, well," Johannes spoke to her. "Uh, this one's okay, I'll take care of it. Thanks Lindsay." He motioned to the secretary, and put a hand behind Miranda's back, and the other hand motioning her to his office. "Please, have a seat. To what do I owe this visit?" He drew all the blinds closed, and locked the door.

"Uh, I just wanted to apologize for how I-well, I was just in the neighborhood, and stopped to say hello." She stuttered. He came in close to her and embraced her, engaging her attention with a long kiss. She backed away, nervously, "What if someone comes in?"

"Oh no, no one bothers me here. I prefer it that way. It makes the clients edgy because they never really know what I'm up to because I usually visit them." He pours a drink, and offers one to her.

"No thank you. I drove myself here."

"I've missed you." He said as he sat near to her.

She felt so bewildered by his presence, reconsidering that maybe this was a huge mistake. He was so close to her now that she could feel his breathing on top of each other. Flashbacks of the night they shared together came flooding back. And as she closed her eyes, she could feel his body pressing against hers again. "I-"

"I know."

"You don't even know what I'm going to say," she whispered hastily.

"I love you Miranda."

He did know what I was going to say. This man is making me lose my mind. "That's what I came to talk to you about. I love you too." she whimpered, as a tear filled her eye. He aggressively kissed her, tugging her hair up behind her with his hands. He trickled his fingers down her neck and to her chest. "No. Not here."

"I have to have you again."

"But, Johannes, not here. We can't-" just as she began to try and convince him this was a bad idea, Gayle burst through the door. Startled, both of them jumped and Miranda covered herself. Johannes stood to his feet.

"How the hell did you get in here?"

"I have a key." Gayle became ravenous. "Who is she?"

"Gayle get out of my office! Lindsay!" He shouted.

"I don't understand what's going on here. Johannes?" Miranda questioned in sheer terror. Who was this woman? Why does she have a key to his office? Was this is girlfriend? Did I just fall into a trap by another man trying to convince me otherwise?

"Miranda, I can explain. Please, don't leave, just wait here. I'll take care of this."

"There's nothing to take care of Johannes." Gayle turned her body and kneeled next to Miranda. "Hi, Miranda is it? Listen darling, Johannes and I are sort of commingling partners. Do you get what that means?" Miranda's eyes widened, and glared at Johannes. "That's right, love. He and I are lovers, I hope you didn't think it was going to be forever between you two. Aww, you did? That's adorable. Johannes, tell her." As she continued, she stopped herself with her revelation she had to share. "Wait a minute... Aren't you married to Victor Setes?"

And in that moment, Johannes took notice of security arriving at the door. "Is there a problem Mr. Oxenburg?"

"Yes, this woman has broken into my office. Please have her removed from the premises, and notify her company immediately."

As they grabbed Gayle, she started to scream, "Johannes, I will tell everything I know! Lockon Properties will pull out of its business dealings with you permanently, do you hear me?! And you, Mrs. Setes, were you aware that your husband is a silent partner in that deal?!" Laughing hysterically, she made one more verbal threat, "Wait until the shit hits the fan folks! This is over! Do you hear me? Over!"

"Um, I need to go." Miranda said, collecting her things. "Obviously you have moved on, and I'm now intervening. I'm so sorry Johannes." Tears streamed down her face as she was filled with embarrassment.

"No, please wait Miranda." It was too late, she was running toward the elevator. Johannes slammed the door shut, and erratically threw his things off his desk. Lindsay, the secretary was shuddering because he had never behaved this way. Lindsay had to find Miranda and tell her the truth about Gayle Lockharte. That conniving bitch has manipulated too many men, and ruined a lot of good things for people.

Lindsay rushed to back to her desk, "Mr. Lockon please. It's urgent."

*   *   *

Lindsay tapped on the door after signs of the deplorable behavior had subsided. Without a reply, she slowly opened the door.

"Are you okay sir?"

With tears in his eyes his only response was, "I have to have her back. These few weeks without her in my life have been abominable." He sat in his chair behind his desk, a grown man crying.

"Sir," Lindsay wrapped her arms around him to help ease his pain, and said, "We'll figure this out."

"Gayle." He said angrily. "That bitch. Get on the phone to Lockon Properties now. Let Mr. Lockon aware of what just happened. Leave out Mrs. Setes. I don't want her drug through the mud with this."

"But sir, isn't *Mr.* Setes known for his endeavors of the illicit kind?"

"Do it Lindsay. Mr. Setes is a subject for another day. Right now get on the main issue at hand."

As he wrapped up that sentence, Lindsay hugged him tighter, and Miranda walked back in the door. "Sorry, I forgot my keys on your desk." Restraining her tears she snapped, "I don't want to interrupt yet another conjugation."

She hadn't wanted to return to the scene of the crime, but considering she had forgotten her keys, she had no choice. "Wait. Miranda, you have it all wrong." Lindsay said, jumping up to calm her. "Johannes loves you! Please listen, you deserve him. He is a great man."

"I just came for my keys." Miranda shunned Lindsay's rational and headed back out, "Johannes, I was wrong to get involved here. I'm sorry."

"Miranda!" He shouted after her. Slamming his fists on the desk, he walked back to his office.

*   *   *

Lindsay whipped around towards her desk to get on the phones. Johannes had pulled himself together and headed home to regroup for the evening.

Upon returning home herself, Miranda was greeted at the door by her husband. Odd, she thought to herself, but brushed it off and gave him a peck on the cheek.

"Where have you been?" He grumbled.

"Oh, I took a drive into town. I needed some fresh air. Why? Is everything alright?

"Oh things are fine. I had a strange call late this afternoon."

"Oh really? What about?" She quandaries.

"An associate of mine, Lockon phoned me. He said that his... Top associate became hysterical, and unpredictable."

"Wow, really? Over what?" Definitely not concerned with what he was talking about, she was sure he was going to mention something about the events occurring in Johannes' office earlier today.

"Not too sure. She was radical, and raving. I think she was involved with the person or something." He eyed Miranda awaiting some sort of confession, and when he had failed to gain any insight on her whereabouts earlier that day, he decided to take a more aggressive approach. "Why were you at Oxenburg's today?"

Completely caught off guard by the directness of the question, she responded, "I wasn't- where?"

"Gayle, the woman who was taken away from Oxenburg's office was apparently so displaced because she claims she witnessed you and Oxenburg together."

"Darling, I don't know anything of the sort. If this woman was as displaced as you say, maybe she is not a reliable source for such idle gossip." Searching fast, she was trying to think of a reason why she was downtown to begin with besides the fresh air thing, and apparently had nothing. "Since we're trying to put the dirty laundry in the open.. Are you having an affair?"

Abruptly caught, he started to choke on his own words, "What? Where are you coming with this Miranda? I have done nothing of the sort!

I will not be patronized in my own house!" He stormed into the study to pour himself a stiff drink. How could she know? There's no way. She's just trying to take the attention off of herself.

She entered his study, and decided to give him one last chance to come clean. "Josie and I saw her at the party. In fact, your female companion and I-unbeknownst to her-had quite an unveiling in the woman's powder room that evening-"

"Josie! This is all coming from Josie! You are forbidden to speak to that wench from now on. That bitch has never liked me, and she is filling fantasies in your head. This conversation is over woman!" He flagged her away with his hand, Miranda stormed off and Victor turned back to his drink. As he slumped into his armchair, he reached for the phone, hesitated to look around the room making sure it was clear and free to speak. He dialed, when a woman answered he began, "Will I be able to see you tonight?"

"Baby, of course you can." She acknowledged agreeably. "I'm yours for the taking baby."

"Alright, give me a few minutes, and I'm headed your way."

Miranda dropped a tear from her cheek as she set the receiver of the phone down. Unbelieving of what she had just heard. Confirming what she already known to be true. What an asshole. How could I have been so naive! Maybe I was the perfect candidate just like Josie had been telling me all these years. Victor just wanted me to be the picture of what he wanted people to see. Quiet, attractive, done as she's told Miranda. Interrupted by her husband, her thoughts subsided.

"I've got to get damage control done for this girl Gayle. She really ripped apart a well-oiled machine. This is going to be in the papers tomorrow, and I need to get a head start." He turned and headed downstairs.

Miranda followed after him about halfway down. He opened the front door, and she yelled down the foyer, "See ya tomorrow... Vic!" His eyes widened knowingly that only his mistress calls him by that name. His look of shock turned to an indisputable rage. He ran back up the stairs and in full confrontation slapped Miranda to the floor.

"Don't you ever talk to me like that again. Do you hear me?!" He yelled in her face. He left slamming the door. She could hear him revving the engine of his Bentley coupe. Screeching his tires as he left in fury. As soon as she knew he was gone, she ran to the phone and called Josie.

"I'm on my way, just keep the doors locked, and if he returns hit him with something." Josie hung up the receiver and raced to Miranda's house.

A knock on the door startled and awakened Miranda from her numbing sleep. Her eyes were puffy from all the crying she had recently endured. Her face had a handprint mark left by her vicious husband. The doorbell rang, and then another knock on the door. Miranda started to feel afraid. What if he came back to hit me again. He had never hit me before. And before she could start manipulating the thoughts in her head from bad to worse, she heard Josie's voice.

"Miranda!" She shouted. "It's me! Open up! Are you ok in there?"

Miranda rushed to the door, opening it, to find Josie, and Johannes standing right behind her. "I didn't know who else to call that would protect you better than I could." Josie stepped aside, allowing Johannes to burst through the door. With a tear in his eye, he inspected my face. His rejoice that I was ok quickly changed to wrath.

"Victor did this to you?"

I nodded.

"Where did he go?"

"Yeah! We'll get this bastard!" Josie was hyped up.

"Josie, we're not going to do anything. Johannes, he was asking me where I was today. I told him I was out taking a drive, and getting some fresh air downtown. Someone called him after Gayle called Mr. Lockon. He told me he had to go do damage control which is why he left, but I heard him pick up the phone, so I picked it up in another room, and listened in." Miranda started to cry. "He isn't going to work." She tried to catch her breath to continue her recount of events, however sporadic they had been. Josie went into the kitchen to make some tea, while Johannes was trying to calm me down.

"Ok, I've got it so far. Just slow down so we can get to when he hit you." Leading her to a nearby chair.

"I heard him say he was going over there-to her house-he hung up and came upstairs to tell me his lies, and as he went downstairs, I called him Vic." Josie came in with the tray of tea and heard this.

"That's what his hussy calls him!" Excited to know she didn't miss a beat while she was in the other room.

"Well, he came back up the stairs where I was and slapped me. Told me never to talk to him that way again."

"So, I don't get it. Who's Gayle?" Josie said confused.

Johannes tapped her shoulder, "Trust me, don't worry about it. We'll let you know what's going on with that later." Josie continued to prepare the tea for everyone.

"I guess he heard I was at your office."

"Because of this, Gayle, woman?" Josie seemed to be finally catching on. Miranda and Johannes nodded.

As they sipped their tea, Miranda started to cry again, and this time, Johannes held her so tight, she was convinced that he truly cared for her.

7
Chapter Seven

As the three of them sat in silence in the darkness, a loud crash was heard from the entry of the house.

"What was that?" Josie hastily whispered.

"I have no idea," Johannes blurted, "wait here." He darted up past the women and into the foyer. With the women shuffling close behind him, he picked up what looked like a large brick with a note attached to it.

"What is that?" And with a usual flair for the obvious she stumbled saying, "A note tied to a brick? How original."

Rolling her eyes, Miranda picked the note from Johannes hands and began to read aloud, "I know your secrets, and I have one of my own! Pretty soon everyone will know all!" With a huge sigh, tears came to her eyes, "Well, someone knows about us." As she looked at him with such sorrow. How did she think she could pull this off? How could she contrive such behavior, and so recklessly? And the brick? Who would be so angry to send such a thing? Cliché, maybe, but in whatever the case still frightening to her.

"We'll find out who this is Miranda. They won't get away with it," Johannes chided.

"It's not just that. Whoever did this obviously knows about us, and is trying to scare us at that. Do you think..?" Miranda sat in questioned thoughts, racing through her mind. Could this be Gayle? What about Victor's mistress? She was so confused at what, or who this could be, that it exhausted her to think any further this evening.

"Hey guys, let's just call it a night, and we'll think some more about this tomorrow. It's been a long day, and I for one and pleased to get it over with." Miranda stated with such intention.

Josie, knowing Miranda for so long decided, what she wants, is what she's going to get. At least tonight. She definitely didn't want to add to any more drama tonight. "Honey, I'll be at home. Call me if you need anything..." as she collected her things and headed toward the door, she hugged Miranda, and insistently repeated to her," ...anything Miranda, I mean it."

Johannes saw Josie to the door, and turned to Miranda, "I'm just going to see her to her car. Make sure it's safe, ok? I'll be back to say goodbye." Miranda nodded, as she watched the door close behind them. The night air was cooler than usual, and had a crisp breeze piercing through it. He looked around them making sure all was quiet, opening Josie's door for her, "I think I'm going to stick around a while, just in case Victor decides to return, or should our friendly brick-thrower decide to toss more things our way."

"Johannes," she looked up from him inside the car, "I'm worried for her."

"I know you are."

"No, see you don't understand," she said looking around him from inside the car to make sure she didn't follow them out as well. "I've known Miranda a long time and..." She hesitated, carefully marking her words. "well, I've just never seen her so alive. I know it's wrong of me to be supportive considering her marital situation; But, believe me, I wish Victor were you. He has treated her horribly for so long-"

"Josie, I-"

"Let me finish."

"Ok. I'm sorry, please continue."

"He's not right for her. He never has been. I guess what I'm trying to say is, please don't let go of her. I want her happy, and I know it's you she's been waiting for all along."

After a moment pause, they smiled at each other, with a silent understanding of what is to come next. He shut her car door, and she started the engine. Waving as she pulled out to the street and drove away. As he turned to walk back up to the house, a dark shadowy figure stopped in his path.

"I should have known it was you." The figure spoke.

"Who's there?" Johannes squinted, trying to look through the light around the figure. Before he could make out who it was, he was attacked. Before he knew it, he was fighting for his life, dodging blows by the fists of this murky silhouette. Out of the corner of his eye he noticed a glimmer of something with a handle attached to it. As it came down toward his face he realized it was a hatchet. Wrestling around on the grounds of the estate, he noticed another sound of screams. It was Miranda!

He looked toward the screams and shouted for her, "Get back inside!! Call the police!" Before he could look back at the figure he had seen what he was to believe was the last thing he'd see in his lifetime. The figure, with a grunt, hit him with a hatchet. Then darkness fell upon Johannes.

*   *   *

An older man is sitting in his wingback chair in the darkest part of his library waiting to hear the news of his latest endeavor.

"Well?"

"All finished sir. Johannes is a thing of the past." A younger, dashing looking man not clear enough to recognize.

"Wonderful. Your account has been deposited with the amount we agreed upon, and I suspect you will be needing this." He hands the shadowed figure a first-class ticket to Greece. He leans back in his chair, taking a puff on a Cuban-born cigar. After a few bouts of silence, he has recognized there is a problem with his new-found friend. "Is there a problem?"

"Actually, sir. There is... You see, if I am to head off to Greece, I am left a little uneasy about how much I had to sacrifice. You could have the Feds all ready to come and arrest me while you sit here with Johannes out of your hair, and me, keeping all those millions you have promised me."

"Mark, it's a shame you haven't come to trust me my boy. I released you from prison, cleared of your crimes, and allotted you a substantial amount of cash to hold you over while we secured the second part of our deal."

"I want another five million." As he walked out of his own shadows and took a seat.

"I'm sorry son, but that's not going to happen. A deal's a deal. I have delivered my part, and now it's your turn. Meaning, take your ticket, and get the hell out of the states."

"I'm afraid I can't do that." Mark Bevent took out a gun, and shot the old man in the chest, just left of his heart. Enough to keep him alive for a slow death. As he was hit with the bullet, he slumped in the chair. If he didn't die this moment, no one could pin his death on him. Mark had learned a few things while being imprisoned. And now, because of Johannes Oxenburg, he was living a life in hiding. He couldn't work for any corporation, his life was ruined. Now that Johannes is as good as dead, and this old man who tried to lock him up again without due payment. No one was going to get him. No one else knows now the dirty deeds he has been up to.

Mark ran around to the other side of the desk. "You listen here old man, no one messes with Mark Bevent. Not even a miserly old grouch like you!" Aiming the gun as if to shoot him again, he rattled off, "you think you can fool me? You think you are going to have me locked up again and keep your money? Forget it. And yeah, I can shoot you in the head again right now, but I want you to actualize the fear that you are actually going to die. Nice and slow." He chuckled. "Stupid old man, oh, and before I forget," he stepped over him, "I need to wire that money to my account. Now, I gave you a chance to hand me 5 million more, but since you've upped the anti, now it's going to cost you ten." With a few taps on the keyboard, the money was transferred, and he slithered out of the old man's office, unnoticed.

8

Chapter Eight

As Miranda leaned over Johannes, she whispered to him that he will be alright. Surrounded by the sounds of the ECG, EKG, life support machines, and a hospital of bustling force, she couldn't help but wonder who on earth would do this to him. Was he involved in illegal matters that would prompt someone to want him dead? Well, she thought, he wasn't dead yet, and she wasn't about to watch him die. "We're going to find out who did this to you," she whispered to him. With that, she left him a gratifying kiss on his forehead, and began to gather her things.

"May we speak with you, Ms. Setes?" an investigator behind her asked.

Startled, she replied, "Of course, sure. Goodness, you caught me off-guard."

"I'm with the San Diego Police Department," he flashed his badge, and took out a notepad, "would it be alright if I asked you a few questions?"

"Uh, yes sure," she stumbled, afraid that they may believe she had something to do with this.

"What was your relationship with Mr. Oxenburg?"

Was? He isn't dead, yet, she thought. A little early to be putting him to rest. She answered in compliance, "A friend. We had met weeks ago, and began a friendship."

"Do you know who might have done this? Was he dabbling in unethical, or unmoral state of affairs? Anything that may be unusual?"

Shaking her head, "Uh, no sir. Like I said, I have only met him recently and was getting to know him. My husband-"

"So, you're married?" The investigator raised an eyebrow, as to suspect the obvious. "Was your relationship more than friends Mrs. Setes?"

"Oh no, sir," she replied, a little more irritated as to where this was going. "I have a wonderful marriage, and women and men can be just friends, uh, sir." She caught herself getting upset, and showing those signs to the officer. She did not want this little thing to get blown out of proportion. "Look sir, I don't know who did this, all I know is that he and my other friend Josie were at my home." Slowing, as to carefully choose her words, she began again, "We were just merely having tea together. All of a sudden we heard a noise. We got up to see what it was, and someone had thrown a brick into my house through the side window of the front door. It had a threatening note attached to it. Johannes walked my friend out to her car, and the next thing I know he is being attacked by some guy. I can't describe him because it was a pretty dark evening. And by the time I called the police he had run off. I came out after calling the police and he was unconscious."

The investigator was writing in his notepad which seemed like an eternity. When he finally looked up from all the notes, he gave her a wicked eye, making her feel guilty, snapping his little book shut, and put it away. "I'll be in touch. Oh, one more thing, how can I get a hold of Ms. Josie... what was her last name? I will need to get in touch with her as well."

"Josie Shirler. She's at 445 Twist Lane."

He put out his hand to commence this conversation, or rather interrogation, has ended.

Stopping him before he exited, she asked "What are the chances of finding out who did this?"

"Ma'am, I will need to corroborate the other witness' story, and possible suspects, then I will let you know. I'll be in touch." With that, he left her sights.

*   *   *

Sitting outside in the gazebo, Miranda buttered her English muffin, while Victor read the latest news headlines: FOUNDER OF LOCKON PROPERTIES FOUND DEAD AT HIS HOME. He let out a disgruntled sigh. "I can't believe this!"

"What is it dear?" She asked.

"Mr. Lockon was found dead at his home early this morning. He was the "Sillent Partner" for this deal I'm working on. With him dead, all my efforts for it are gone! That son of a bitch!" Angrily he dropped the paper onto the table, and looked out across the lawn.

"A man is dead, and you're concerned with his corporation's financial interest? Seems a little upside down in thinking, don't you agree?" she was confused. She knew how important money was to him, but to know of a man that has just been slain? It didn't sit right in her stomach.

"Do you realize how important this is?" After a short delay, he continued rather maliciously, "No, I guess you wouldn't understand. All you worry about is your charities, and your designer clothing. So, go on worrying about that. But, since I am the one funding all those luxuries, a dead man, is a man I can't do business with Miranda."

Unsettling as all this sounded to her, she couldn't blame him. She was still upset about Johannes. He still lay unconscious and all she was concerned about was him. She hadn't heard from Josie either. Interrupted by her thoughts, Victor continued reading the article aloud.

"Says here he was found dead early this morning, but was dead far before anyone had noticed him missing. He tended to go into hiding from time to time, so that wasn't so unusual. But, his assistant hadn't been able to get a hold of him...It says Gayle, yes, Gayle Lockharte had been trying to get a hold of him for almost two weeks."

Gayle Lockharte. Why does that woman's name keep coming up? It was all Miranda could do to get that nasty woman out of her life. Maybe she had something to do with his murder? And the attempted murder on Johannes? Or maybe she was just a dumb slut who kept turning up at the wrong place and time? It would deem obvious that a woman like that was capable of murder. Maybe she didn't exactly murder him herself-no, that wouldn't make sense. That jeopardizes her monetary interest. With Lockon dead, she would have to find another job. Unless she was put in the will.

There's a motive to be found there if that is an accurate concern. Maybe she should call the investigator and give him Gayle's name.

*   *   *

After romping beneath the silk covers at her posh apartment in the city with Vic, she just couldn't believe how lucky she was. She was going to marry such a prominent man of business, have a family, and live happily ever after. Of course, after he gets rid of that wife of his. Now that her little boyfriend is left for dead in the hospital. And she now knows about her, things are starting to move into her favor. Mrs. Bianca Setes. It has such a nice ring to it. Better than Miranda, she thought. Miranda could never compare to her exotic looks. A red-head, and a brunette. No comparison. Once Vic realizes that Miranda is cheating on him it will all be over. She watched Vic as he rose from the sheets. "Do you think Miranda would ever cheat on you?"

Angered, he turned quickly toward her, "Don't you ever mention her name from your lips again."

"It's just that, I really want us to get married, and I don't want anything getting in the way of that. I want to start our life together baby." She batted her eyes at him, hoping to help sway him towards her thoughts.

Longingly, with a look a father would give his daughter, he sat next to her for a moment holding her hands in his and said, "Look, honey, maybe I can't leave her. I'm not sure I will be able to. I have been with her for too long. And, there's so much for me to lose if she decided to be vengeful about me leaving her."

This not only pissed off Bianca, but enraged her to the point of boiling hot water. She calmed herself, and instead of going on about this, began to fondle Vic. If there was one thing she knew, it was that keeping a man happy in the sack and giving him too much sex would definitely persuade a man to do whatever a woman wants him to do. After their bouts of sexual pleasure, she prided herself on knowing that he may not want to leave his wife out of formality, but getting to know Gayle Lockharte is definitely going to come in handy again.

After Vic left her place, she darted to the phone. "Gayle, hi, its Bianca. Remember what we talked about? Well, yeah, I think we're going to have to move to Plan B."

* * *

"Do you think he's going to wake up anytime soon?" Miranda heard a voice speak from behind her. She turned from Johannes bed and saw Lindsay, his assistant holding a box of candy for him. "I brought him a gift. I hoped you'd be here. Can we talk Miranda?"

Still angered by everything that has happened, she couldn't possibly speak to another one of Johannes' lovers. Not now. Not ever. She was so insane with jealousy by every woman that came into their life. Mostly, in part due to the facts of their dramatic relationship and the bullshit they've endured since they've met.

"Miranda, I promise you, Johannes and I, we're just friends. I work for him, and that's all it's ever been. No I'm not married, nor do I have a boyfriend. But, I do know what it means to a woman to be in love, and by that, I can see how much in love you are with him. We women, we've got to stick together. Because once in a while, there's that bitch that comes along trying to destroy everything in her path. In our case that bitch is Gayle. Everything she does is motivated by her need to get ahead for herself. She'll sleep with anyone to make a buck, or get a house, or shoes. You're a threat to her. She is lacking what you have. Johannes made a mistake by sleeping with her, he knows it, and I hope you do too. He is in love with you, and I know you've been here almost every day, and that tells me you're very much in love with him." They both sat in silence just staring at him in the bed. Lindsay put the gifts on the bedside table, and brushed his hair with her fingers. Turned toward Miranda again and continued, "I just hope you realize what a great catch he is. I'm sorry things happened the way they have, but you have to believe what I am telling you." Lindsay finished, turning once more before she left the room, "I know you may not trust anyone right now; But, I can help you with your marriage." Miranda looked at her, deep in thought. "I know some things that will help you, and Johannes specifically told me to take care of you if something happened to him." Turning her back to Miranda, she headed out the door.

"Lindsay," she bolted up from her seat, "Wait! Please." Lindsay stopped from exiting the room, and turned to face Miranda. Miranda rushed up from her chair beside an unconscious Johannes. Reaching for Lindsay, she began, "I am sorry Lindsay. I am so confused, and I am in love with Johannes, and I shouldn't be. I should never have even met him, then none of this would have ever happened. I..." She stopped herself, not wanting to relive their most passionate moments. "My husband's having an affair."

"I know."
Shocked, Miranda replied, "You do? But, how?"

"It's easy to find things out when you have friends in high places."
She smiled. "You know, you need to get some fresh air, let's have lunch."

Pulling up to an upscale restaurant, they walked up to the hostess, "Table
for two please."

"Right this way Ms. Lindsay," The girl happily greeted. "It's so
great to have you back!"

They sat at a table, partially secluded from the main room. "Your
table," she motioned, still smiling. Miranda couldn't take her eyes of the
girl. Something about never breaking from that smile creeped her out.
They sat, and Lindsay nodded to the hostess as she gave them their menus.

"Do you come here often?" Miranda quandaries in friendly
sarcasm.

"Oxenburg holds a lot of business meetings here. The food is
lovely; but, that hostess is annoying." Laughing as they glanced over their
menus.

"Your husband." She glanced down, and back to Miranda's eyes
with all seriousness, "I think he had something to do with this, among
other things."

"Among, what other things?"

"I think your life may be in danger as well."

"Wait, you think my husband.. Hold on. He may be cheating on
me, but he would never--" Miranda trailed off, racing through thoughts in

her mind that her own husband may actually have her killed. "But, he could just ask for a divorce." She stated so sadly.

"I know, it seems it would be that easy; but, your husband isn't the type of guy that likes to lose. And divorce says you lost at the game of marriage." Lindsay quickly blurted, "I have someone investigating your husband. I'm sorry, I should have told you sooner, but when all that went down in Johannes office with, well... you know, I just knew there was trouble brewing."

"Maybe Gayle had something to do with this?!"

"No, she's a tramp, but that doesn't give her a motive to try to have Johannes killed. There's something else going on." Setting her menu down as she noticed the waitress approach, she happily demanded Miranda, "Now, let's eat!"

9

Chapter Nine

Without hesitation, Gayle hung up with Bianca, and picked up, dialing a distant relative. "Yeah, Plan B. Yeah, I'm sure. The cops were here questioning me about Lockon."

"Just stick to the plan, and move cautiously. Go about your normal routine, and it will blow over," The man grumbled on the other line.

"Bianca is already to move, and with Johannes in the hospital perfection couldn't look so beautiful!" Gayle hesitated, "What about that Miranda woman? She's been around Johannes a lot, and I think we can sink her by bringing that information to Victor."

"What information? There's no proof. Get it in print honey, and we'll deal with that. I don't think we'll need to worry about her much anyway."

"How can you be so certain?"

"Because, she may not wake from her bed tomorrow morning..." Giggling in prowess over his plan.

"I underestimated you handsome," pleased by his unburdened logic. "I've got to get moving, I need to make some purchases." Gayle hung up the phone, grabbed her keys, and headed out the door.

                    *   *   *

Leaving the restaurant, Lindsay and Miranda parted ways. "Thanks for everything Lindsay. I don't feel so alone in this anymore." Miranda's thoughts were aloft and chaotic. She just knew there was more to this story than meets the eye. "I'm just an exclusive member of the housewives club, never a mother-although I've always wanted them. I know Gayle has something to do with this. Why is all this happening to me? I just wanted a faithful husband, and a charmed life I could grow old in. Gosh, I must sound crazy, a middle-aged woman walking around talking to herself." Her mind, all over the place was causing a flurry of emotions. A disturbance of any sensibilities she thought she'd had. And Johannes. Why would someone want him killed? What did he have to do with anything? Did Victor know of the affair? Could he have done this? Why would Victor care about the affair anyway, He had Bianca. "Bianca," Her lips pursed and her temper flaring. "Home wrecking slut." Bianca-who he was planning on a new life with when he hadn't closed the chapter on the old one! "Didn't I deserve the respect of being 'let go'?" No. She thought. I am the dumb, naive housewife. Mumbling aloud, she was getting a good look at the sidewalk when she suddenly bumped into the woman in front of her. "Oh, I am so sor-"

"Hi, Miranda, isn't it?"

"Gayle Lockharte."

"Well, what brings you here? Coming to get a gift for your lover?"

Enraged, she spoke out of her better judgment, "You stay away from him, you.. You witch!"

"Ha ha," smirking, " I knew you two were sleeping together. What do you think your precious Victor will do when he finds out?"

"He would never believe what comes out of your mouth."

"Oh no?" She paused, "You keep on believing that," she moved in closer within inches of Miranda's face, "because, honey, I know everyone's secrets. Including your unconscious boyfriend's. It's a shame he was beaten in front of your house that night, I wonder what the neighbors must of thought of that?" Raising her brow, as she turned to walk away. "oh, and by the way. Your husband is lunching with his girlfriend." She strolled away as if she had a skip in her walk. Pointing in the direction of the popular sushi spot, 'Ra.'

Miranda sporadically looked around in hopes no one had heard their conversation. She rushed by the window to glance inside the restaurant, sneakily as not to be noticed. And she saw them, Victor and Bianca, together, sharing a dessert. "Could my day get any worse?" She slowly crept away from the direction of the restaurant, and headed home. What did she mean by Johannes' secrets? She knew Gayle was in on this; But, Miranda knew she didn't know that much about him, but he would tell her anything. Wouldn't he?

*　　　　*　　　　*

Josie had been trying to get a hold of Miranda for what seemed like an eternity. She was knocking on Miranda's door when she finally answered. "Good gracious girl! Don't scare me like that! I've been looking for you all day."

Miranda motioned for her to come in. Although, Josie had already taken the initiative of waltzing in before being asked. She figured the formalities between them are long gone. They've known each other for too long. "This was on my desk at work today, I didn't know what it meant. And, I don't know who sent it either. Would you take a look at it?" As she handed the note to Miranda.

EYE YOUR LITTLE FRIEND
FOR SHE MAY NOT LIVE
TO SLEEP ANOTHER WINK

"What the hell is this?" Miranda asked her shockingly.

"I don't know, that's why I thought I'd show you."

"Who sent it?"

"I already told you that I didn't know. I went to lunch and there it was, on my desk when I returned." She stated matter-of-factly, "I tried to call you all day."

Miranda didn't know what this meant, but for some obscure, and uneasy reasoning, she believed this was meant for her. "I think Lindsay was right."

"What? Who?"

"Lindsay, Johannes' secretary. We had lunch today after I visited Johannes at the hospital. Anyway, she told me that she believes I may also be in danger, that not just Johannes was targeted that night."

"Why would someone want you.. I don't understand all this?" Completely confused, Josie was up pacing the floor of Miranda's kitchen. "Here, I'll make us some tea." Unsure of how to take all this information. Shaking her head she said, "This is like some crazy movie!"

Miranda started rattling off all that has happened since she'd seen Josie, and Josie was intent on trying to keep up. The sound of the teapot whistling startled them both, and Miranda got up from her chair, to turn off the burner. Getting the cups from her cupboard, and placing tea bags in each cup, she continued on while Josie sat with a blank stare on her face trying to make sense of it all. "Josie, I just am starting to feel like this is all my fault."

"First of all, sit down." Josie got up to grab the honey, and some spoons as Miranda brought the teacups to the table, setting them in their respective place settings. "None of this is your fault! Hear me right now, Victor cheating on you is his fault, not yours. Johannes getting jumped in front of your house is not your fault. Gayle, well that piece of work, is her parents fault, and we're going to figure this out." Taking her seat again, they properly sweetened and stirred their teas in silence. Both heavily in thought as to what to do next. Josie set her cup down on the saucer, and began, "Ok, this note. If it were meant for you, then what do we need to do to protect you? Where's Victor?"

"He called and said he was going out of town on business, he said he had what he needed and didn't need to stop at the house."

Josie rolled her eyes, "Ok, so let's start with making sure everything is locked up tonight, and let's change your alarm code."

Split between her fear, and her overreacting, Miranda wasn't sure how much she really needed to do here to protect herself. If that noted really was for her, then she needed a little more than a wood door and a little lock on it to stop this person from hurting her. As they finished their teas, they went around Miranda's house checking off all the places that needed extra bolts, or locks. After helping Miranda make her house a little more safe, Miranda walked her out to her car.

"Oh, and you're going to need this too," Josie said pulling out a baseball bat, and handing it to Miranda. Miranda eyed her like this was overboard. "You never know, just put it beside your bed where its easily accessible, and just remember to use it if you need to." Miranda took the bat, and they hugged each other.

"Thanks Josie."

"If you need me call me, I've got a date!"

"I could never keep up with that girl." She smiled to herself.

Later that night after she had bathed and watched a little television, she checked the house one more time through just to make sure everything was locked. She went upstairs into her bedroom, and locked her bedroom door, jamming a chair underneath the doorknob. She lay in bed, scared out of her mind, but reassured herself that she was just overreacting. Tomorrow she would go to the police with the note, and let them know of her suspicions. And with a little more surety that this riddle will get solved, she drifted off to sleep.

10

Chapter Ten

Startled awake by a noise, Miranda attempted to leap out of bed. Only to be found underneath a large shadowy figure above her, dressed all in black with only his eyes shown through his mask. She struggled to get him off of her, and began to scream. He put his hands around her neck choking her until she started to see everything go black. He let go of her, as if to play with her, allowing her to catch her breath. Then smuggled her with a pillow, suffocating her once again. Flailing her arms, she hit the man with her fists in his crotch, causing him to bend over enough for her to shove him off of her. She jumped out of bed, racing for the door, and he grabbed her by one of her ankles, causing her to fall to the floor. She was shaking her feet to get them loose from his grip, kicking and screaming at him to leave her alone. When he let go with one of his hands, she broke free of his grasp and kicked him in the face, hearing a crunching sound. She bolted for the door opening it. As she went through the door, he came with a bound behind her, slamming her to the floor once again. This time, he grabbed her by the hair, pulling her head back, and held a knife to her throat, "You thought I'd make it that easy for you bitch." Just as he went to slice her throat, there was a megaphone voice coming from outside.

"We've got the house surrounded. Come out with your hands up!"

How the hell? The man thought. He yanked her head back even further back, "This isn't over. Your life is mine." He used his hand that had her hair firmly gripped in his clutches, and gave her head a couple of whacks to the floor, cutting her face on the floorboards. She lay there lifeless as this evil man jumped out her window. As he made his escape, the police broke through her front door, looking up to see her laying on the stairs lifeless.

"We're going to need an ambulance here." The policeman stated over the walkie talkie to headquarters.

*   *   *

The next day, almost a month to the day of Johannes accident, he finally awoke from his coma. With the nurses around him elated, the doctor was to visit him shortly to check his vitals.

"Welcome back Mr. Oxenburg! We were starting to wonder about you." The doctor cheerfully explained. "Are you able to sit up for me? I am your doctor, Dr. Rembo." Helping Johannes from his usual sleeping position was tough. "After a month of lying flat, it would prove problematic to get those muscles moving again." The doctor chuckled, "Don't worry Mr. Oxenburg, you're a healthy young man-a month of Sundays shouldn't affect you more than if you sat around being a couch potato all month." Dr. Rembo was a short, stout looking man. Balding on top of his head, you can tell he isn't yet convinced that he's losing his hair because he is trying to comb the hair on the side of his head up and across the top. He wears his stethoscope around his neck, as most doctors do, and has thick glasses that keep falling down his nose.

"Doc, when can I get out of here?"

"Whoa there, not so fast! You need to go through physical therapy, and we need to get you an MRI so we can check for other possible nerve damage. You had quite an opening in your head." He started writing on his chart, "If I didn't know any better, I think somebody was trying to kill you Mr. Oxenburg," he chuckled.

"You don't say?" Johannes said sarcastically, "Thanks."

"I'll be back to check in on you after your MRI. We can let you know from there where you're at recovery-wise, and about how soon we could get you out of here." Dr. Rembo looked again at his chart, writing some more, "In the meantime, hang in there, watch some television." The doctor grabbed the remote, and flipped the television on, "Tell me how that Megan Mullally show is, you know the lush from that show 'Will & Grace', I haven't yet seen it." Out he went.

"Great.." Johannes quipped, throwing his head back on his pillow.

As he flipped through the channels all he could think about was how people could really spend their day watching all this crap they put on TV. It's just amazing, he thought. "Maybe if I was a pregnant housewife." He turned off the TV and tossed the remote back onto the nightstand. As he readjusted himself in his bed, he looked up and saw Mark Bevent standing before him.

"I heard about what happened, and I just wanted to come by and see how you were doing."

"I thought you were locked up, they let you out on good behavior?"

"Yeah, something like that." Mark knew this wasn't going to go well, Johannes still resented him for stealing from him, and with due course. He was responsible for multiple off-shore accounts, and not only did he mishandle them, but he embezzled millions that could never be recovered. Mark was jailed under suspicion of this act because they could prove he had a huge role in it, but could never find the laundered funds. "Look, I understand that I'm the last person you'd ever want to see, but I wanted to personally apologize for everything."

Something wasn't right about this visit. How could Mark be out of jail, even if it were good behavior, he wasn't up for parole for another eight years, it had only been two years. Nobody's that good in their attempts of reform. If he was to wonder more about Mark, there was the issue of why his nose was bandaged up. "What else do you want Mark?"

"I am supposed to deliver a message."

"Oh, it wasn't that you were sorry for everything you meandered?"

"Well, sure, that. But, Mr. Lockon was found dead in his study, about a week after your accident."

"It wasn't an.. Accident. Someone attacked me, Mark. Is that all?" Just wishing Mark would leave already.

"No." Mark hesitated, "Well... here." He took out a piece of paper and handed it to him.

YOUR NEXT

"What the hell is this?" Confused by what he was reading, he had thought this might have been a random attack, but seeing this in writing he was sure that he was a target. A candidate for murder. "Where'd you get this?"

"On my way here, an old man handed me this after he asked who I was going to go visit here. When I said I was coming here to visit you, he handed me this and said pass it along to you."

"Was this the same person that told you about Mr. Lockon?" He asked, still in profound shock that Lockon was even dead. That old bastard could outlive an atomic bomb.

"No, I read about it in the Business section." After a long silence, Mark walked closer to Johannes to give him a shoulder tap to encourage him. "I hope you recover. I'll see you around bro."

"Yeah, yeah." What the hell was going on here? I was attacked, Lockon is dead, Mark is all of a sudden out of jail--all this in one month?! This is nuts. Johannes could not believe what was happening. Someone was after something. And he had to figure it out. Was it for money? Likely. Power? Possible. Love? Victor. Was Victor trying to scare him away from Miranda? Did he know about them? Would he actually take it as far as to have him murdered to do it? Unlikely. Either way, something needed to be done, or it couldn't be done from this damn hospital room! "Nurse!"

Miranda, Josie, and Johannes sat at Miranda's kitchen table watching the news, "CEO and founder of Oxenburg Investment Enterprises, Johannes Oxenburg, was released today from Tri-City Hospital. While, still at large, his unknown attacker has kept our police detectives extremely busy. Since the attack, it has been reported that there are multiple threatening notes warning the corporate executive to 'watch out'. Police suspect this case to be very dangerous and have put select members of their SWAT team on as Mr. Oxenburg's personal bodyguards until further notice. As for the description of the attacker, he was rather tall, dark, and shadowy." Miranda flipped off the television.

"Tall, dark, and shadowy? That's the best they could come up with?" Josie, in her usual sarcasm continued, "For a news team, you would think they'd have come up with a better description."

"It's what we described at least..." Miranda grinned, shrugging her shoulders.

Johannes glancing out the window grumbled, "How long do these oafs have to baby sit me. Do they really think it's going to stop these people?" Shaking his head, "I'm a big boy!" He yelled at them through the window. He returned to the table with his coffee cup in hand.

A knock on the door came with a thunderous sound and they all turned to look at each other. "Who could that be this early?" Miranda asked.

"I'll get it!" Josie jumped up, anxiously vying for something to do. She bounced out of the room to get the door.

With a rush, she returned with Lindsey. Lindsey had her arms full of all kinds of papers, and folders, and she was talking so fast, she could possibly out run a train on its tracks. "I found out who's after you. I've got documentation, facts from the police department, my own investigator has been working around the clock, following around who we suspect is trying to kill you."

"Who?" Johannes jumped, "Who the hell is trying to kill me?"

"Ok, get this, Victor," She glanced at Miranda, "your husband, is sleeping with a woman named Bianca. Bianca is friends with Gayle. My P.I. was tailing them separately until he noticed they were having little meetings together. Gayle and Bianca were plotting against her boss, Mr. Lockon, using him to get money. Lockon would give Gayle a $20,000 dollar a month allowance, not including a credit card with a $100,000 balance. Every time Gayle's payment was registered to her account, half of it would get re-deposited into Bianca's account. These two have been stock-piling money like this since Gayle started sleeping with Lockon. And if you haven't done your homework, that's-"

"Eight years.." Johannes, deep in concentration, affirming what he's hearing.

"Right. Not including the money they would cash out from the credit card. According to Gayle's credit card statement, she would take a cash advance every month or so in increments of ten to twenty thousand. The card would get paid back by Lockon's advisors, and would never question her about her expenditures. After interviewing his accountants and such, it came back that they figured Gayle was his trophy girlfriend, and she got whatever she wanted, and in the beginning when this started, when they would go to Lockon about her spending habits, he would state very clearly that they are never to question him about her habits. She gets what she wants because she was his girl. Obviously confirming why they shouldn't question him. Every six months or so, the money accumulated in her accounts would be redirected to an off-shore account in Greece. I can only assume that she was going to do this with him as long as necessary and when he finally kicked the bucket she was going to move there and be happily ever after."

"But, Lockon's dead now. She no longer gets an allowance without her lover being there to hand it to her, right?" Josie asked.

"Yes, and no. In his will, three-quarters of his estates to her, all stocks and bonds to his company to do with what she will, and the other quarter to his acting chief executive who was not named in the will. Ordering that the remainder of his business merge with a company called Bevential Communications."

Johannes shook his head, "Never heard of it."

"Me either. Whoever killed Lockon knew something, or just got greedy. In his computer records, about the time he was killed, he made a transfer of funds to an account in Greece. We couldn't trace the account holder's name, but somehow I think Gayle has something to do with this. I don't think she murdered Lockon because she was getting what she wanted, and I can't figure out what having you and Miranda as targets fit into this at all."

"Well, Gayle is definitely suspect in my book. What are the odds that Lockon makes a transfer of-how much was transferred?" Josie phlegmatically positioned.

"Millions." Said Lindsey.

"Exactly, why would he transfer millions to an account in Greece, which indirectly connects Gayle, and then he dies?"

The four of them sat there, heavily thinking about what was all just ingested. Could Gayle really be a killer? That woman could be awful, but a killer? Cross-referencing all that was said between them. Did the police know all these things? If they had known, they more than likely would have brought these people in for questioning.   As they were sitting around contemplating back and forth, entertaining conversations over what to do next, an officer came into the house with a guest.

"Victor!" Startled by the audacity that he would dare come back to the home where he had put his hand to her. Miranda became uneasy but contained herself, "What are you doing here?" The rest of them turned around to see Victor standing there with an arrogant presence.

Victor cocked his head up high, and squared his shoulders as he noticed Johannes seated at what he believed to still be his table. He gave a glare accompanied with an evil grin towards Johannes.

"Victor." Johannes said his name, more sure now that he was his enemy, rather than friend.

"Johannes, I must say. I am quite surprised to find you here. Trying to save the day, are you?" He leaned in towards him and lowered his voice to Johannes, "How's my wife?"

Johannes jumped up and grabbed his shirt collars, pulling them up and aggressing him into the door frame of the kitchen entry, "You bastard."

"Stop it!" Miranda shouted. She raced to the other side of the table to intervene. As she did so, the armed Swat member cocked his firearm, shouting to the men orders to back down. Johannes looked at the cop, then to Miranda and the fear in her eyes, and he let go of Victor, backing away from him.

"What are you doing here Victor?"

"I heard Johannes was released and wanted to ensure he was alright."

"We both know that's a load of shit!" Josie blurted.

"Hi Josie." Victor turned back to Miranda, "I came to make a deal with you. Can we talk in private?"

"Whatever you have to say, you can say here."

"Ok, then. I want to make this work with you. I made some mistakes, but there's too much to lose if we put ourselves through a divorce. The media would create a circus, your image with your charities could take a hit, and-"

Shaking her head, "Victor, I know about Monica."

"Bianca!" Josie corrected.

"Right, thanks Josie. It doesn't matter what her name is. The fact is, I know about her. I also know that you care about yourself. The media not making you look like a fool, and you're worried about the financial end of this divorce. I know you could truly care less about me-isn't that why you hired a hit man to kill me?"

"What?! I did not hire any hit man!" Victor was getting angry. He didn't hire the hit man, that's for sure, but thought more of these attacks as a good wake up call for her and Johannes anyway. He wasn't exactly opposed to having these two... 'off'd.' It would make his life a little simpler actually.

"Victor, we are getting a divorce," and it was as if she could read his thoughts, "and it's too bad for you because I am not going to be murdered any time soon." Miranda gave an eye to the officer, and he escorted him out.

"You're not going to get a penny, you bitch! I know you're type, I made you! You're nothing!" Miranda and the rest of them could hear his muffled threats even after the door shut Victor outside. They gave themselves a good laugh, and patted Miranda on the back for sticking up to him. And, for the first time in her life, Miranda actually felt a sense of freedom come across her entire being.

"Feels like a huge weight has been lifted, hasn't it?" Johannes closed in near to her.

Feeling his arms wrap her tightly, she drew a huge breath and let out the greatest sigh of relief. "Oh yeah, bigger than any brick."

11

Chapter Eleven

That night, Victor was drinking himself into a stupor at a bar in a ritzy restaurant. He couldn't help but moan on and on his complaints to the bartender. "My wife is going to try to take me for all I have. That bitch. I... am going to show her. I have the best lawyers in town. Her little perfect wife image will be shot when I show the world about her infidelity!"

"Sir, I can understand that you are upset; But, dude let's try to keep it down-for the guests here trying to enjoy their dinners." Although, he had to keep to rules, he wanted to hear more about this guy's problems. He leaned in over the counter, "So, your wife, why did she cheat?"

"Well, it's a little complicated," hesitantly, Victor chose his words tastefully, "She found out about my mistress."

Eyes wide, he stammered a chuckle, "You mean to tell me, you're cheating on your wife, and when she found out, she cheated on you? That's classic!" The bartender had a surfer look. Since the restaurant was overlooking the beach, the bartender was a surfer-type with blonde hair, cut with a shaggy look the kids all seem to be sporting. Very reminiscent of the character Shaggy on Scooby-Doo.

"I gave that whore everything!" He angrily whipped his drink into his hand, gulping down more liquor. "She used me. That's it, she thought she'd use me for all my money, buy her stupid clothes, and chapeaus..." He glanced around the room, lowering to a whisper, "Hey, if you ever get married, watch out for those gold-diggers. They will try to take you for all you got." He slammed his empty glass to the bar.

"I don't think I'll have that kind of money any time soon. It would be gnarly though. Would you like another?" Nodding, Victor pushed the empty glass for a refill.

NEWS REPORTER TALKING: Today, Victor Setes was removed from his home in the upscale neighborhood of 'Seven Bridges' near Rancho Santa Fe by police. He was said to be violating a restraining order picked up by his wife. It is unknown if any violence had occurred at the residence; But, it is certain he won't be visiting the Mrs. Any time soon."

"Killer dude, you'd think a guy like that would just take it up in court. Instead he goes back to the scene of the crime." Shaking his head smirking, the bartender wipes down the bar.

"Hey! I didn't touch that bitch!" He stood, his voice barreling over the low restaurant noise. Quieting, the diners all stopped and looked in their direction.

"Sit down man." Reaching to tug at his elbow, and motioning for him to return to his seat. "It's alright folks, please return to your meals." The bartender gave him wide-eyed encouragement, and Victor sat back down at the bar-stool.

"Look kid, thanks. If you ever want a real job, give me a ring. I'll put you in the right direction." Victor stood and wobbly headed out the door. His driver, waiting outside, opened the door to the limousine and ran over to Victor to help him into the vehicle. Victor slumped in his chair, and the driver opened up the partition.

"Rough night, sir?"

His eyes blurry, he could not see the driver very well. In his attempt to speak, all he could manifest was a drunken nod. Raising his hand, at his second attempt to speak, all went black. The driver's eyes in the rear-view mirror, he pushed the button to initiate the partition closed.

*   *   *

Back at the bar, the bartender was on the phone, "Yeah, hi, I work here at The Chart House, and that guy that was on the news for beating his wife? Yeah, well, I think that dude was just here! Yeah, he was so wasted out of his mind! Yeah, I'll be here till Midnight man." He hung up the phone and went on about his normal business.

NEWS REPORTER BEAMING: "I'm here outside The Chart House, an upscale restaurant in North County where it seems Victor Setes has thrown a belligerent rage against this young bartender. Would you go into detail about the violence against you?"

"I, um, he didn't attack me." Pushing the microphone from his face.

"When he struck you, did you know he was one of the richest men in San Diego?"

Squinting from the shining lights of the camera, he responded, "No, I didn't know him except from the news reports. He just rambled on, like most of our bar patrons do."

"So, I guess you could say that , part of your job is sort of like a therapists?" She glimmered. "More on this breaking story later. This is Judy Choo-signing off!"

The cameraman shut off his camera, and began wrapping up cords, and headed to the news van. "Thanks kid, this guy is going to go down."

Feeling a bit guilty, he asked the newswoman, "Why did you tell the public that he like, uh, smacked me? That's not what happened."

"Oh honey, you're adorable. Don't worry, the public doesn't care whether he hit you or not. He has already beat his wife, and has a mistress. This is just icing on the cake."

"But, you're kind of ruining his life."

"He's done that on his own. Thanks for the story kiddo!" she started to shuffle away, and turned back to tell him, "If you have any other info, just call me!"

"Yeah, thanks." He put his head down, and walked back into the restaurant.

*   *   *

The doorbell rang at Bianca's door. Dressed in a satin nightgown and high heels, she made her way to answer it. "Who is it?" Noticing how late it was, it couldn't be Victor.

"It's me."

Quickly she opened up, "what's the matter?"

"Sorry it's so late, I wouldn't have come if it weren't important. Here, help me get him in here."

To her horror it was Victor. He lay lifeless in the hall of her building. "Oh my God!" She rushed in with her visitor to help lift Victor off the floor. Dragging his unconscious body into her apartment, tears started to stream down her face. "Is he.. Dead?"

"No, he just drank too much."

"Did he notice you driving the limo?" She asked.

"No. The last thing he did was raise his hand, and then passed out. Anyway, we have bigger problems." He said, removing his gloves and hat.

"Yeah, I know. I saw the news."

"The news? What are you talking about?" he worried.

"He hit a guy in that restaurant we all used to go."

"He what?! I can't believe this!" He started pacing the floor, working the gears in his head to figure out what to do now. "If he doesn't stop this maniacal behavior, he's going to get us found out!"

"He's just doing what he knows brother."

"He's going to screw everything up! This is a delicate situation."

"I know, I know." She said softly, stroking Victor's head. She got up and went into the bathroom. Grabbing a washcloth, she rung out some water, and returned to Victor's care.

He went to the phone and dialed, "Yeah, get to Bianca's. Our delicate flower Victor was up to his disastrous ways again."

"Help me get Victor to the bed, will you?"

"Let that bastard lay on the floor. He's no good to us." he glared.

"He's good to me!" She pleaded, "I love him, Mark. Please help me get him to the bed."

With a grunt, he helped her. As they lay him on the bed, there was a knock on the door. "I got it."

"Oh baby," she said embracing Mark in her arms. "It feels like its been forever."

"Soon enough we'll all be in Greece, lying on the beaches, touring the country sides."

"Ahem." Clearing her throat, realizing that apparently they have forgotten she was in the room. "Remember? Big problems at hand?"

"Hi Bianca." Gayle shifted her eyes with disappointment. "Your little boo-boo bear go comatose?"

"He had too much to drink." She muttered.

"Look, I think we've all got enough money to carry us for quite a long while as it is. Let's just cut our losses and get the hell out of here now." Mark said.

"We can't. The estate hasn't been settled yet. Once I get all Lockon left me, we can get out of here."

"What he left-you."

"Us. I meant, what he left all of us." She forced a smile. "Are you saying you don't trust me now Mark?"

"Well, it's funny how things are getting pretty hot here, and you want to 'wait' things out. We don't have time. The plane tickets can be traced, you're in the will, there's too many variables linking us to Lockon's murder."

"It's all circumstantial sweetheart. They can't pin something on us if there's no viable proof." She scooted off to the kitchen to pour herself a cocktail, "Besides, the media seems to be focused on Mr. Setes' drama anyway." She motioned her glass to Victor and Bianca. "The one we have to worry about spilling all she knows is right in front of us."

"I wouldn't tell anyone anything!"

"Doubtful. But, we'll keep our eyes on you at any rate." Gayle shot down her drink.

"I just want to spend forever with Victor." Bianca said longingly towards his inanimate body.

Mark and Gayle looked at each other, laughing. Leaning in to kiss one another. "To forever!" They said in unison, toasting their empty glasses. Caressing each other inappropriately.

12

Chapter Twelve

Back at Miranda's house, the private investigator was tearing through Victor's library. Flipping through papers and tossing books off of shelves. Lindsay was talking to Johannes as they were paging through mountains of files. And Miranda could hear Josie running through the house like a headless chicken. Probably enjoying every minute of the idea that she's turned sleuth detective. Miranda could do nothing but feel anxious that Victor would return to the home. She proposed that maybe it was one thing that people were after Johannes. After all, she didn't know him all that well. But, he seemed such a real and genuine person. Unless he ran into some people that were just not right in the head, or were that jealous of him... People were trying to kill her though now too? What did she ever do to anyone? She played the good wife all these years, did her charity, was involved in the community... none of it seems to make any sense!

Lindsay and Johannes stopped silent for a few pauses, and just looked shockingly at what they had stumbled upon.

"Miranda..." Lindsay hesitated, "Take a look at this."
"What... What is it?"

"It looks like an insurance policy that was just taken out on you only a few months ago." Lindsay stated.

"Well, we've always had our lives insured. He is very prominent in our community, as am I, so we just thought it'd be safer to make sure..." she trailed off. What? Wait a minute... Why would he... "How much was it for? And how long ago was it redone?"

"Well it says here that it was done about three months ago, and your life, or upon your death rather, would be worth 50 million dollars."

"50 million... American dollars??" Miranda stuttered.

"What?! Who insures people for 50 million dollars?!" exclaimed Josie. "You know what I could buy for that much? Alright that's it, Miranda, drink this poison!" Josie in her usual bad timing and taste, says jokingly.

Johannes shook his head, trying not to show his smirk at Josie's comment, although it did lighten the mood of the room. "The only reason anyone would take out that much on a policy is to cash in on it," he said, turning his gaze to meet Miranda's and noticing her face losing it's vivaciousness and turning a pale shade of bile.

"I agree." Said Lindsay, turning to the P.I. She asked him, "What do you think, Lou?"

Looking up at all of them, he nodded, and went right back to shuffling through Victor's desk. Stopping short, he noticed something under the desk. "Ladies and gentleman, I think we have another lead." They all rush to take a look underneath and gasp at what they see.

Awakening to a heavy knocking on the door, Bianca slipped out quickly to answer it so she wouldn't wake Victor who was sleeping off his liqueur induced coma. Opening the door she found herself staring at Miranda Setes. "Uh, um... May I help you?" Startled and unsure of how she got her address or even knew who she was.

"I believe we need to talk." Miranda demanded and started to push her way through the door.

Stopping her from coming in, she hurriedly pleaded, "I know, I know. Please, not now. Um... Uh, can you meet me in an hour? He's here now, sleeping off some alcohol," keeping her voice hushed, "please, I am so sorry, just please, meet me in an hour?"

Miranda was furious and wanted to deal with this now, but realized this little Brazilian girl obviously had a conscious, or at least some sort of compassion to the duress of the entire situation here. She hated how beautiful she was with her gorgeous dark hair, and big puppy eyes. "Fine. There's a coffee shop on 3rd and Market. Meet me there in an hour. Or I will come back. With the police."

Bianca was freaking out, trying to get herself together and get out of her apartment before Victor woke up. How could she get so mixed up in all this? Getting involved with a married man, and then Gayle and Mark... Killers. They were right about her though, she needed to get this shit out of her life. She just wasn't cut out to lie and kill. And, then lie about killing.

"Look, I know you're doing my husband. I didn't want to know, so I was in denial for quite some time... I'm sure it's been months, and truly, I just don't really want to know the actual time you two have been cavorting." Miranda stated assuredly. Staring at this young girl, almost young enough to be her daughter, Miranda could see the naiveté with this girl, and almost feels sorry for her. But, then doesn't.

"I'm sorry Miranda. When I realized it was you I was talking to in the restroom at the banquet, having a face to a name actually hurt me. It made me feel so remorseful about what I've done to you and your marriage. I am very sorry, but I must also let you know the truth. I am in love with Victor, and I can't let him go. I want to spend forever with him."

Hearing this killed Miranda inside, but she also knew that after what Victor's done, there was no going back to that anyhow. "Look, I cannot say we will ever be friends. You can understand that." She gave a short smirk to Bianca, and Bianca returned a kind smile to her, knowing that naturally, that will absolutely never happen. "But, I do need your help now. And, I need you to be on board here."

Looking down into her hands, "They think I'm weak; that I will run to the police..." Bianca sullenly admitted, "I know about who's plotting to kill you. And..."

Giving her a motherly look of endearment, reaching for Bianca's hands, Miranda said, "Thank you. I think if we work together we can take these people down. We need all the help we can get and I will contact you as soon as possible with what to do next. Also, I'll notify the investigators that you're on our side so that they can amp up your protection just in case."

"Ok. I will help you."

*   *   *

Back at Miranda's home the next evening, she sat with Josie, Johannes, and his assistant Lindsay. And Bianca. Awaiting the arrival of the private investigator. Everyone is silent. Looking around the room awkwardly at each other. Josie leans in and whispers, all too loudly, "I think we should kill her."

Bianca shoots a nasty glance toward Josie. "I hear you."

Josie says, "I was hoping so."

"Would anyone like a drink?" Johannes offers; but, no one obliges. Finally, a knock on the door is heard as they all jump up from their chairs, startled. "Guess we're all a bit jumpy." He chuckles.

"Miranda, I don't trust her! This is just another game of hers to save herself," complains Josie.

"She's the only one who knows they're plans and what really happened. Let's give her a chance." Miranda lets the detective inside. "Any news?"

"Ma'am... we've got a problem. Someone pitches a brick through your window; yet, there's no fingerprints or witnesses. Just a man with a hatchet wound-"

Josie giggles at the way the detective chooses to describe Johannes' attack, as Miranda shoots her a glare. "Sorry..." She attempts to stop her laughter and shuffles back to her seat. "Sorry."

"As I was saying-"

"Detective, this is Bianca. Victor's, uh... mistress." Miranda turns to Bianca, "Is that what, I mean, is that ok? Sorry, I don't know what you're title is..."

Ashamedly, "That's fine, Miranda. I understand... just keep that one away from me." Bianca points to Josie, as she looks at Miranda and whispers, "I think she really does want my head on a stick."

"You betcha! Ho!"

"Josie!" Miranda interjects. As the two women start to argue and move towards each other.

"Now. Now! Knock it off..." said the detective. "I like a chick fight as much as the next guy, am I right?" He elbows towards Johannes in a boy's club fashion, and continues, "But we have a murder, an attempted murder, a hottie mistress, hellooooo..." giving a bow to Bianca, "and I have a hankering for a taco. So, listen up! We are going to take all your statements, Ms. Flip Flop over here is going to give us everything she knows and we will file your case accordingly."

"So, how long will this take, officer?" Lindsey offers.

"As long as it takes, ma'am... for me to grab my taco. I'm starving."

Johannes exhales. "Oh geez."

* * *

Johannes walks towards Miranda in the foyer and puts his arms around her. "How much longer is this going to take, Johannes?" she begged.

"Looks like he's wrapping up with Ms. Flip/Flop..." they both giggled. After a pause, he continues... "Do you think she can be trusted?"

She lets out a gasping breath, "I have no idea." Shaking her head, "It seems like the people I've trusted can no longer be trusted and the people whom I never thought cared, have cared more for me and, I don't know, everything is just so topsy-turvy. I really don't know what to think anymore."

"I think, we should keep an eye on her. I'm not 100% certain, she's entirely on our side yet. She seemed to want to help us so easily, no?"

"Yeah... she did." Miranda falls into Johannes' chest and hopes that she isn't wrong about Bianca.

"Alright kids, I'm done here. If there's anything else y'all need or want to ask, feel free to ring me up," skips the detective. "It's going to take me a couple days to sort all this mess out. But, I'll reach out to ya when the dust settles, alright?" he states rhetorically, as he walks out the house.

Johannes follows the detective outside, "Detective, come on, a couple days? We know Bianca has to know enough to get an arrest on Victor, right?"

"I'm sorry, Johannes. But I can't di-vulge what hers, or anyone's statements to me. Those were in confidence and when I get everything fixed up... I'll give y'all a shout." He plops down the stone steps and looks over his shoulder, "Hey, uh, Jo-haannes?"

"Yeah?"

"You wouldn't happen to know where the nearest taco shop is, would ya?"

Disgruntled, Johannes resupplies, "When you head out towards the freeway, there'll be one on your right. Can't miss it."

"Alrighty! Thanks! Y'all have a good night," as the detective skips off, Johannes is can feel the indignation rising inside of him. He can't just sit back and wait for Officer Aardvark to solve anything while he's on a taco gallivant. He's determined to find out who did this to him. And find out who killed Mr. Lockon. He has a feeling, whoever's behind this is clearly seeking revenge. And they aren't taking any prisoners. They're planning to exterminate anyone in their path.

13

Chapter Thirteen

Back in the office, Gayle is straddling Mark on his office chair behind the desk. Her skirt is pushed up, on top of her hips; exposing her ample derriere to the cold breeze from the outside window behind them. His hands are caressing up her back as her slip is falling from one shoulder. Gripping the skin of her back underneath the silky sheath, his mouth is buried in her neck, as his arms pull her in tighter to him. She rocks her hips, harder to feel his cock go deeper inside her and as he's gripping her closer to his chest, she throws her head back and moans loudly. Unafraid of any passerby's on the street below will hear her. He slides his arm up her back, still under her blousy tank, up past her neck and reaches for a tight grip on her hair. She arcs her back and moans, louder still. He whispers, "this what you need baby..."

"Uh... huh..." breathlessly she responds.

"Daddy going to take care of that weak link for you?"

"Yes. Yes! Fuck me, daddy," she demands as she looks him in the eyes. "Fuck me... "She exhales, "Fuck me and kill that little whore."

He grunts aggressively, as he pulls he hands from out of her, now wrinkled undergarment, and uses his hands to pull her down by her shoulders into him. "Come for daddy... Come on baby. Show me you want this. You want me to take care of business." As he pants intermittent gasps of air, he commands her to submit herself to him. And his direction proves successful, as he speaks, and sinks her body into him by his control, she begins to come all over his cock. Screaming loudly in pleasured desire. They breathe heavily, in unison, as he confirms for her, "I will right the wrongs that were done to me. With you by my side, Johannes Oxenburg's empire will fall. Even if I have to take out every last person connected to him."

Gayle devilishly giggles at the thought as she rises up off of Mark's lap and pulls her skirt down and readjusts her other clothes. After they're both dressed they are seated in the conference room discussing the next phase of their plans. "I don't trust her."

"...And that's why, YOU, my darling are going to kill her," said Mark.

"What? Me?"

"You're going to have some drinks. You're going to dump this little pill into her glass. You'll eat, you'll dance... You know, play along as if all is normal." He carries on and smirks, "forty-eight hours later... she chokes expectantly, far away from you. She will most likely be with Victor, that alcoholic joke and he will watch her die."

"Oh... you are a devil." Gayle climbs slowly across the table, with an evil grin and his tie in her grasp.

"Not now. We have work to do." He hands her the pills and shoves her away.

Miranda and Josie arrive at Miranda's house to an onslaught of photographers and news reporters. Josie is pushing them through the sea of chaos, with a closed fist, punching her way through, left and right. "Move the hell out of the way, fuckers! No comment! Go home!" As they shove their way into the foyer, Josie slams the door in the intruder's faces, "Criminy, you bastards just don't care about privacy, do you?!" She turns around to a horrified Miranda, "What?"

"Ugh... nothing. Absolutely nothing..." Miranda exhales as she removes her scarf and throws it on the table, in the center of the floor. She turns to Josie and expresses her disdain, "I just couldn't have imagined that it would have ended this way... I mean, come on... assassination attempts on my life? Johanne's life? Maybe your life now..."

"Come on Miranda, first of all. I'm too much of a badass. No one is going to kill me." Josie jokes. "Secondly, we are going to figure all this out. I know it doesn't feel that way now... but, it will be fine. Good always finds a way to triumph over evil, right? Right. So, let's entrust the cops are doing their due diligence and they will catch these assholes. All of them. However many are involved."

"Maybe you're right." The women move to the kitchen and Miranda starts to make a pot of tea. "Good will triumph..."

"Now, I have some ideas about who's after you. And Johannes..."

"What happened to entrusting the cops?" Miranda queried.

"Ha! Trust the cops... that's a good one. They'll be a latte and two scones in before they even come close to figuring this out." Josie blurts flippantly. "Besides, that half=wit detective wouldn't know a crime scene if he saw one." The teapot whistles and Miranda collects the cups and pours the water. As Josie steeps her teabag, she notices something in the stairwell and starts to walk towards it as if she were in a trance.

"Josie? Josie... what is it? Are you ok?"

"Do you see that?" Josie asks Miranda. Miranda shakes her head slowly, unsure of what Josie is doing.   As Josie leans down next to the staircase, she uses her shirt to pick up a cufflink. Miranda and Josie both look at each other in shock, confused by what they've found. "Maybe it's Victor's?"

"No. I've never seen it before... "

"Maybe it's Joha-"

"I'll ask him. It must be, right?" Miranda concludes.
"I don't know... didn't the intruder try to throw you down the stairs or something? Or fought with Johannes in the foyer?" Josie is going over the possibilities.

"What home intruder wears cufflinks?" Miranda looks at Josie. "I think we need to call the detective."

"Don't. You. Dare! That idiot doesn't know his ass from a hole in the ground. I got this."

"What are you going to do?"

"Don't you worry... I know exactly what to do." Josie tosses the cufflink in the air and catches it with one hand and storms towards the front door.

"Josie... What are you doing?"

As Josie grabs the brass handle, she turns her head back to Miranda and winks, "Trust me." She throws open the door and shouts to the reporters, "You morons want something juicy?! Look at what I got for ya." Josie holds up the cufflink in-between her fingers, displaying it for all the media to gawk. As she had hoped, they rush up to the steps of the threshold and start snapping pictures, asking a multitude of questions. "You got a picture of that?! Good! You tell the owner of this piece of jewelry that we know who you are and we are coming for you! No more living in fear. You don't scare us anymore. If you come after us again, you are as good as dead! And by the way mother fucker, we dare you!" She turns around abruptly, entering back into the house, slamming the door. With a quick sigh, Miranda meets her gaze.

"What the hell did you just do...?" Miranda stated rhetorically, fear in her eyes.

"We just changed the game, girl. You're intruder is going to see that and believe we already know who he is; even though we don't. He'll either run scared or come pining for us even harder."

"Yeah, now you'll have a price on your head too, Josie. Why did you do that?"

"Because you're my best friend. My family. And no one messes with my family." Miranda shudders a laugh as Josie puts her arms around her. Miranda knows this isn't going to be good and while Josie's right that she changed the game by pulling that stunt, Miranda's fearing that Josie really has no idea what she's just done at all.

*   *   *

Bianca is nursing Victor back to health at her apartment when she hears the new anchor talking about Victor's wife on the television. She scoots to the edge of her bed and lowers the volume to watch the report. Looking back to make sure Victor isn't hearing any of this:

"Today, a startling development in the Setes case. An unnamed woman announces today that they know who the intruder, now is, and plan to aggressively prosecute. Notice in the tape, the woman is holding a cufflink, which is presumably believed to belong to said intruder."

Bianca turns off the television, as she hears Victor moving around behind her. She is startled by her phone ringing. "Uh, hello?"

"Hey, it's Gayle. How are you feeling? Is Victor doing better?"

"Uh, yeah, he's been in and out of it. Detox is not a pretty sight."

"Well, hey, it's been pretty tense lately... Let's get drinks. Only if you're up to it."

Relieved, Bianca responds, "Absolutely. "

"Bartender, two cabernets, please." Gayle requests, as she and Bianca get settled in their seats at the bar. "Whew. We really needed this, huh?"

"You have no idea..." Bianca responds, haphazardly, unsure of why Gayle has brought her here. She never considered Gayle a close friend; in fact, she's almost certain Gayle can't stand her. Maybe she's had a change of heart. We are all knee deep in some pretty terrible shit and no one else could possibly- crap. Bianca is hoping Gayle doesn't suspect that she's gone and talked to Miranda.

"Hello?"

"Oh. Huh? Sorry..."

"Did I lose you in a daydream?" Gayle jokes, forcing a smirk.

"Um, yeah, I guess so..." To distract from her thoughts, or tipping off Gayle, she grabs her glass and motions for a toast. "To us! Our future on the islands together!" The women clink their glasses and in unison, "Salut!"

"God Dammit!" As Mark throws his remote across the room at the television. He starts pacing the room. Thinking of what to do next. If they know his identity, then he can't carry out his mission... Unless... Maybe they don't know my identity, he thought. "It's a fucking cufflink. That isn't going to lead them-fucking cufflink." He starts racing around the room, throwing clothes into a duffle bag.

*   *   *

Gayle and Bianca have been chatting it up for hours at this point and Gayle is getting perturbed that Bianca hasn't once looked away from her cocktails. Gayle just needs six seconds to drop the tab into the glass but waiting for Bianca to distract her gaze has been agonizing for her.

"Would you excuse me? I need to -"Bianca starts and Gayle quickly jumps in.

"Absolutely darling! Go ahead, I'll order us one more before we close it down for the evening."

"This has been really great. I needed this, thank you Gayle. This was a nice change of pace from all the chaos that's been swirling around us." Gayle nods in acceptance and tilts her champagne, mimicking another toast to Bianca as she saunters off to the bathroom. As soon as Bianca is out of sight, Gayle drops the tablets into Bianca's newly served glass before she returns. "Ah, much better." Bianca sighs as she returns and plops back down onto her chair.

"Cheers! I ordered us one more for the road." Gayle devilishly knows this is it. This bitch will be dead tomorrow.

"Thanks Gayle, but I believe I've had enough. Here's some cash, sorry, I'm just exhausted." Bianca retorts. Gayle is fuming and knows this is her chance to finally off this stupid whore.

"Oh Bianca," Gayle over-exhorts, "don't be a buzzkill. One more and we'll get you home."

"I appreciate it, I truly do. This evening was much needed but I'm plum tuckered out. Talk to you tomorrow." Bianca has never been so assertive with Gayle before and she knows she's gotta get out of here before she catches on that she spoke with Miranda. Gayle must know. Maybe that's why she's pushing me to drink some more. Hoping that I'll spill this secret that, maybe, she already knows. Keep it cool, keep cool, she calmly thinks to herself. She stands up and grabs her bag, "Thanks so much Gayle! Toddles!" She hightails it outta three with a cherry demeanor hoping Gayle didn't suspect anything. But, Gayle is pissed beyond recognition and realizes something, Bianca has never told me no. Just as she swigs from her glass, she glances at the television and hears the news reporter: WITH NEW EVIDENCE, FOUND AT THE SETES HOME, POLICE BELIEVE THEY CAN TRACE THE VIOLATOR OF MIRANDA SETES BY THIS CUFFLINK. EARLIER TODAY, A REPRESENTATIVE FROM INSIDE THE HOME, BRAVELY WENT OVER THE AIRWAVES, TO SHOW EXACTLY WHAT OUR PERPETRATOR HAD LEFT BEHIND. I DON'T KNOW ABOUT YOU BOB, BUT THAT LOOKS LIKE A STYLE YOU WEAR. The reporter chuckles and hands off the next segment to Bob. Whom laughs it off as he begins his sports report.

"Shit." Gayle slams her glass to the counter and reaches inside her handbag for her phone to get Mark on the line but he doesn't answer.

14

Chapter Fourteen

Gayle reaches Mark's apartment and he appears to be gone. His place looks like it's been turned over by mobsters and there's even broken glass on the floor. "What the hell happened here?" She mumbles beneath her breath. She keeps trying him on his cell and it's now going directly to voicemail. "I can't just sit around here and wait, he must be planning to leave without us. He must've seen the breaking news report." Gayle rushes out of his place and heads directly to Bianca's. But no one is answering at her place either. "I was with her barely an hour ago and she said she was heading home," Gayle thought. She tries her on the phone without success. "What the hell is going on? Why has everyone suddenly vanished?" She even attempts to reach Victor. She thinks to herself for a moment and realizes she forgot to check Mark's office. As Gayle heads to his work space, she tries him on all his lines, still no answer. Driving herself crazy with the possibilities.

*   *   *

At the police station, Miranda, Josie, Bianca and Johannes are being questioned by the sergeant.

"That detective that's been snooping around for tacos, I don't trust him. Something's not right with that one," states Josie to the sergeant.

"I can assure you madam, all my officers are of the highest selection."

"Right. The highest selection..." Josie mumbles sarcastically.

Miranda jumps in, "So, sergeant, how does this work then? We found this article, clearly belonging to the intruder of my home and no one else we have questioned has claimed it. We are on the right track, right?"

"Well, we can't rule out anyone who isn't claiming the item, ma'am." The sergeant takes a sneering glance toward Johannes. Miranda and Josie look at each other and before one of them could open their mouth to defend Johannes...

"You hold on there, Mr. Chang.
Everyone turned and looked towards his direction, his voice was rather louder than anyone of them would have imagined. But the situation at hand demanded that they did so. They all suspected each other, it was obvious that one of them was not telling the whole truth. One and all of them.

* * *

Taxi! Taxi!! Taxi!!! She yelled and waved both hands, jumping at intervals to show the cabbie that she badly needed a ride.

"Jefferson holdings..." Gayle said as she tries to place herself on the seat just behind the driver. She couldn't really define what she was wearing, she never thought about it. How could she? Thoughts of being cheated and abandoned plagued her heart and only Mark was in the position to relief her of her fears. She hopes to see him.

"Why could they have abandoned her? At least they should have paid attention to her version of the story. But Mark... we had a deal"

"Here we are Ma'am, have a great day" the driver said but she didn't hear him.

"Jefferson holdings right?" he called out again to be sure.

"Ma'am!!!"

"Oh! Sorry, my bad!" she jolted back to consciousness.

She stepped out the cab in a rather dramatic fashion. She placed her leg gently on the pavement as if the ground could open up and swallow her. Gayle stayed at distance and stood in front of Mark's office looking rather puzzled. In a bid to escape the trailing dust, she quickly slips through the door but she is not quick enough to prevent the dust from entering along with her. The hall was lightened up and quiet, and this was not helping her situation at all. Her heart throb was getting louder. She gets an elevator, no sooner had she punched in the floor she desired to access than a young man stepped into the elevator with her. He was holding a flower base, composed of an irresistible variety of blossoms, one that Gayle could not get her eyes off.

"Hi"

"Hi"

She responded the way the young man greeted. That way, they won't engage in an unnecessary conversation. She approached Mark's department. The hall was as large as the reception at the ground floor, except that the paintings were different so also was the floor tiles. As she turned to his door to turn the nob, she wouldn't want to knock, she hopes to get him unawares. Her hands were already on the nob when someone taps her shoulder slightly.